Hometown Star

JOLEEN JAMES

Happy Reading!
Joleen James

HOMETOWN STAR

Copyright © 2012 by Joleen James

This book is a work of fiction. Names, characters, places, and incidents are the product of the author's imagination or are used fictitiously. Any resemblance to actual persons, living or dead, business establishments, events, or locales is coincidental.

Printed in the United States of America

ISBN: 1491001208
ISBN-13: 978-1491001202

Other Titles by Joleen James

Falling For Nick

Under A Harvest Moon

Hostage Heart, *a short story*

Dear Reader,

My love affair with Alaska began on my honeymoon. While vacationing in Alaska I fell in love with the endless summer nights, the incredible wildlife (imagine eagles, bears, and the best fly fishing ever!) and the breathtaking scenery. I knew that one day I would base a story in this beautiful state. *Hometown Star* is that book.

I was lucky enough to spend time in Seward, Alaska, the town used in this story. While writing Hometown Star I tried to stay as true to my memories of Seward as possible. To that end, I'd like to thank my friend Katrina and her parents Steve and Colleen (Seward residents for many years) for their help with all the questions I had. Any inaccuracies with the setting are totally my own.

I hope you enjoy Star's and Cade's story. After all, who doesn't love an Alaska man?

Happy reading,

Joleen James

This one is for all the smart, talented women in my life. You lift me up!

CHAPTER ONE

August
Seward, Alaska

Starlene White stared at the rundown double-wide trailer. Wide stripes of rust ran down the cheap aluminum siding. Dandelions and chickweed grew to the tops of the skirting— well, what was left of the skirting.

She drew in a shaky breath as she mounted the rickety porch steps, the rotting wood giving way beneath her brand new designer sandals. The front window near the door was broken, the remaining glass so smeared with dust she couldn't see inside.

With a steady hand, Star inserted her key into the lock, but she didn't need it. A mere touch pushed the door open. An unlocked door didn't surprise her. Patsy had never locked the door. Why would she? Who in their right mind would want to go inside? It was Star's "city" mind-set that told her to use the key.

Star stepped into the mobile home. The stench of mold and stale cigarettes wrinkled her nose. An instant, vivid image of Patsy, sitting at the kitchen table, a cigarette dangling from her fingers, a can of Bud Light in front of her, flashed through Star's mind. Star closed her eyes, absorbing the memories of a woman more precious to her than her own mother.

"Patsy, you deserved so much better than this place," she said to the room, hoping her aunt could hear her. "I miss you. What am I going to do without you?"

Sadness squeezed Star's heart. She forced the pain away and walked across the avocado shag carpet to the kitchen and hit the light switch. Nothing. No power. Disappointed, she checked her BlackBerry. *No Svc* flashed on the screen. No power. No phone or Internet reception. She couldn't wait to get out of Alaska and get back home to Seattle, to civilization.

For a minute she considered taking her sister, Brandi, up on her offer to stay at her place in town, but just as quickly Star pushed the idea away. If she stayed on site she could wade through Patsy's things in the evening after she finished working for the day. Her on-location job as a production manager for the cable television show *Update This!* came first, settling Patsy's estate, second.

In the kitchen, Star set the bag of groceries she carried onto the counter, along with her purse. She went to the window and turned the hand-crank, hoping for a cross-breeze. A clatter down the hall brought her around and sent her pulse racing. An animal? Probably. Star fished around in her purse for her pepper spray. In the back of her mind she wondered if Patsy's gun was still in the old hatbox in her bedroom closet.

"Is anyone here?" she asked. "Anyone? I have pepper spray and I know how to use it."

An empty silence greeted her. Most likely it was a little mouse, more afraid of her than she was of it.

Feeling slightly ridiculous, Star moved cautiously down the narrow hall, her heels tapping on the yellowed linoleum. At the bathroom, she paused, peering inside at the avocado green sink, toilet, and tub. All clear. That left the two bedrooms.

"Hello?" She paused at the door to Aunt Patsy's room. The bed had been stripped bare. A lump formed in Star's throat. How many times had she crept into this room to cuddle up with her aunt, needing the kind of grownup mothering her own mother hadn't been able to provide?

A ruckus pulled Star around. Before she could react a small boy ran smack into her.

"Hey," she cried, dropping the pepper spray. Her hands shot out to steady him.

"Let me go." He jerked away, running for the door.

Star considered giving chase but quickly discarded the idea. She didn't need to know why the kid was here. She didn't care. Kids were nothing but trouble with a capital T. Raising her three sisters had cured Star of ever wanting children of her own. She never dated men with children. She didn't care how hot the guy was. Kids were a deal-breaker. Period.

A howl sounded out front. Noisy crying followed.

Star sighed. So much for letting the kid go.

She made her way to the open door. The boy lay face down in the dirt, his sobs muffled by the earth. One of his shoes sat a few feet away. Had he tripped on his untied shoelaces?

Star walked gingerly down the steps and dropped to her knees beside him. "Where're you hurt?"

She judged his age at seven or eight years old. Shaggy black hair hid his face from her. He pushed to his knees, then sat back onto his butt.

"Are you okay?" she asked. Dirt streaked his face. Blood oozed from a cut on his lip. "You're bleeding."

He wiped his mouth on his shirt sleeve.

"Let me see." She reached for him, but he scooted away. "Come inside. I'll clean you up."

He shook his head.

Star changed her tactics. "That's right. I'm a stranger. No wonder you don't want to go inside with me, but let's be fair, you were in my house."

The guarded look didn't leave his eyes.

Star tried again. "Let me introduce myself." She smiled.

"My name is Star. Patsy Cooper was my aunt. Well, she was my mother's aunt, and my great aunt. Did you know Patsy?"

He nodded enthusiastically, his eyes lighting up. "Star's a funny name."

"Tell me about it," Star said. "My mother is the Queen of White Trash names. We all have them. My real name is Starlene. My sisters are Ruby Sue, Tawney, and Brandi."

"What's white trash?" He cocked his head to the side, as if he were trying to figure her out.

"You're lookin' at it, kid," she said with a half-grin. "Well, maybe not so much anymore. I'm still white but not nearly as trashy." Star pushed to her feet and bent to dust the dirt from her black slacks, frowning when she spotted the layer of dust coating her expensive sandals. "Come on. Let's go inside and get you cleaned up before your mother sees you."

The boy stood. "I don't got a mother. Not anymore." He retrieved his shoe, shoving his foot inside.

"No?" she asked, curious. "I'm sorry about that. Do you have a dad?"

He nodded.

"You going to tie those shoes?" Star pointed at his feet.

He shrugged but did as she asked, making two neat bows.

Satisfied he wouldn't be tripping again, Star started for the steps, the boy on her heels.

"Let's fix you up for your dad," she said. "Then I'll walk you home. I'm assuming you live around here. I need to find a phone so I can call the power company. Maybe I can borrow yours?" At the sink, Star moved to turn on the tap, but remembered without power there'd be no water. Instead, she removed a bottle of water from her grocery bag. She twisted off the lid, then wet a cloth.

"Let me see your lip. I used to be good at this kind of doctoring. It's been a while, but I think I can remember how to give first aid."

The boy stood still as she washed the blood from his lip and the dirt from his face, a cute face, a familiar face. Twenty plus years rolled away. She knew his face, had seen it on another boy long ago.

Star's stomach plummeted. "What's your name, kid?"

"Finn."

"Finn what?" He flinched when she scrubbed too hard at his lip.

"Finn O'Brien."

Star's fingers tightened on the rag. *The kid was an O'Brien.* Suddenly she was twelve years old, just off the school bus, racing for home, but Cade O'Brien had blocked her way. He wouldn't let her pass. She'd had to pee. She'd given him a shove, but he was older, stronger. He'd laughed at her, asking her why she was in such a hurry to get home to her white trash aunt. Star could still remember the warmth of the pee running down her legs, still remember the smile slipping from Cade's face. He'd let her pass after that and she'd run all the way home, cleaning herself up, telling no one about the intimidation.

Just thinking about Cade O'Brien made her blood boil. Was the kid his or Ron's? What difference did it make? An O'Brien was an O'Brien. As far as she was concerned, they were all as rotten as the wood on Patsy's porch.

Star tossed the washcloth in the sink. "There. I think I have some bandages. Wait here."

In the bathroom, she found the bandages, but when she returned to the kitchen, the boy was gone.

"Finn. Where are you?" She went to the front door. "Finn, are you out here?" Star scanned the yard but didn't see him.

A thick grove of spruce and hemlock trees separated Patsy's place from the O'Briens. Did she have the nerve to go over there? She needed a phone and they were sure to have a landline. It was either face the O'Briens or drive the ten miles back to Seward where her BlackBerry worked.

Cade and Ron O'Brien had made her life a living hell each time she'd come to stay with Patsy, especially Cade. To this day, Star had no idea why he'd tormented, teased her, bullied her. Eventually, Ron had grown up and ignored her, but Cade had continued to insult her with his slow roving stares and smirks. Star stepped outside and pulled the door shut on the mobile home.

She straightened, the familiar control returning. Cade O'Brien didn't intimidate her anymore. She wasn't anyone's charity case now. She was an educated, powerful, career woman, a woman who could take care of herself.

She wasn't afraid of Cade O'Brien.

Not anymore.

* * *

Cade O'Brien raised the ax over his head then let it fly. Razor sharp, the blade sliced through the log with minimal effort, the double-thunk of the two halves hitting the ground satisfying.

He paused, using his discarded T-shirt to wipe the sweat from his face, arms, and torso. He tossed the damp shirt onto a nearby log just as his eight-year-old son Finn burst through the trees. When Finn saw him, he skidded to a stop, then slowed his pace, practically dragging his feet through the grass. His chin came up, as if he dared Cade to question him.

"What's going on?" Cade set the ax down and waited for Finn to come to him.

"Nothin'," Finn said, his eyes fixed on his dirty tennis shoes, *tied* tennis shoes.

"Nothing?" Cade asked, instantly suspicious. Finn never tied his shoes. "You came tearing out of those trees like you did the time you set the woods on fire. What're you up to?"

Finn shrugged, his eyes still south.

"You haven't been over to Patsy's place again, have you?"

Finn didn't reply, his refusal to answer telling Cade everything he needed to know.

"Look at me, son."

Finn lifted his chin. Cade took in the cut lip, the dirty knees, the tied shoes.

"What happened, Finn?"

"I fell."

The kid's face was too clean. His nose had a shine to it.

Cade's eyes narrowed. "Who cleaned you up?"

Finn's chin jutted out. "Me."

Cade didn't buy a word of the story but decided to let Finn off the hook. He was tired of fighting with the kid, tired of trying to keep him away from Patsy's, tired of trying to figure out what the heck the fascination was with that dump of a mobile home. "Why don't you go inside and see if your Aunt Trudy needs help with anything."

Finn took off past him like a rocket.

Cade turned away, his gut telling him he should go after his son and press him for more info, yet he didn't; he couldn't. The kid had a way of looking at him that made him feel like a failure. And maybe he was. Never in his wildest dreams had he thought he'd ever be a single parent. Single. Alone. So alone.

Cade picked up the ax, his hands tightening on the handle. He let the blade fly, again and again, until his arms strained in their sockets. Sweat raced down his face. His breath heaved in his chest. He paused, enjoying the pure physical release of chopping the wood, a release he needed. He needed more; needed...he didn't know what he needed. Cade buried the ax in a stump.

Maybe he needed a break. The scent of fresh baked bread called him to the house. Cade swung around, intending to snag a slice. He took a step then froze.

A woman stood at the edge of the tree line. A beautiful woman. Recognition flared, like a white-hot flame in his gut. Starlene White. He'd know her anywhere. The thick, blonde hair. Those cool green eyes. That killer body.

Star had finally come home.

She started toward him, her shoulders back, her head high. Cade didn't move, couldn't seem to remember how. She wore a crisp white blouse, black pants, and high heels. He took his time taking his fill of her, just like he always had. Her skin was still creamy and smooth, her lips full and so pink he ached to kiss them.

Only he wouldn't. He'd never kiss Starlene.

Battle lines had been drawn between them years ago and he didn't blame her for hating his guts.

* * *

Cade O'Brien.

The jerk.

Star's stomach did a crazy flip flop. Why didn't he like her? She could see the same insolence in his eyes, see it in the stiff, unwelcoming way he held his body, a great body that was wasted on a guy with zero personality.

She stopped in front of him. His eyes did a slow rove clear to her toes before settling on her face.

"Star," he said. "You got the letter."

Seconds passed, the familiar tension rising between them thick and ugly. "That's right." Star lifted her chin. "I got your eviction notice." The pain in her stomach increased. She pressed a hand to her midsection.

"Our attorney advised us to send the letter," Cade said. "It's nothing personal. We're planning on expanding the Bed & Breakfast, building a second home where Patsy's place is."

He stared at her mouth, and that bugged Star. It wasn't the first time he'd done it.

"Patsy's lease was terminated with her death," Cade continued. "Our attorney wanted us to be clear with your family before we demolished the trailer. I'm sure there are mementos inside your family wants."

"How considerate," Star said, her tone even and smooth. "Brandi's coming by tomorrow to help me pack. Believe me, the faster I'm out of here, the better. I'm not staying in Seward one second longer than necessary."

His brow creased—with relief? Star couldn't be sure, but Cade definitely gave off a vibe that said he'd be glad to see her go. Well, she'd be glad to go! Seward, Alaska was everything she'd spent her twenties running away from. I mean, what was there to do here? Nothing but breed babies and choke on the stink of fish. No, thanks.

"If there's anything I can do to help you speed things up,"

8

Cade offered, "I'm happy to help. Patsy was a loyal, dedicated employee of the B & B and O'Brien Charters. I'm sorry about her passing."

"Are you?" Star couldn't resist asking. There was no love lost between the O'Brien boys and her aunt. Never mind that Patsy had worked like a slave for the O'Briens after Cade's mother had died.

"Of course I'm sorry," Cade said again. "For you and your sisters."

Star stared at him, those cold blue eyes of his on her. What did he see when he looked at her? A poor white trash girl, wearing dirty clothes, her hair uncombed? Inside Star shrank, but just as quickly she remembered who she was now. She was the bigger person. She was in control.

"Thank you for your condolences," she said. "Actually, I'm in need of a phone. My BlackBerry doesn't get reception here."

"Sure." Cade snagged his T-shirt.

Star got a good look at his rock hard abs, the abs of a man used to doing physical work. He pulled the shirt over his head, covering all that bare skin.

"Follow me," Cade said.

He strode to the house at a breakneck pace, Star struggling to keep up with him in her high heels. When they reached the front door, Cade held it wide. She passed by him into the house at the same time Finn plowed right into her.

"Whoa," Cade said, catching hold of the boy's shirt. "Slow down."

"It's you." Finn backed away from Star while staring up at her.

"Hello, Finn," Star said, smiling. "Twice in one day. Do you always move at warp speed?"

Finn shrugged.

"You've met before?" Cade asked. "Wait, Star's the one who cleaned you up, isn't she?"

Finn's eyes widened.

"I warned you to stay away from Patsy's place," Cade said,

the words stern.

Finn's lower lip stuck out, wobbled.

Star had heard enough. She'd been on the receiving end of Cade's temper too many times to count. She stepped between Cade and Finn. "He's a little boy. He got hurt. I helped him. End of story. There's no need to get angry."

"He shouldn't have been there," Cade said. "It's dangerous. The place is a decayed wasteland."

They were nose to nose. Star could smell him, pine and sweat, and fresh air. Testosterone to the max. Unnerved, she stepped back.

Instantly, Cade's face softened and he swore under his breath. "The phone's over there." He pointed to a table pushed up against the wall, then turned to Finn. "I'll talk to *you* later."

Finn scampered away out the front door.

Star marched over to the phone. Cade hadn't changed at all. He'd used intimidation on his son, the same kind of intimidation he'd used on her when she'd been a kid. Nothing made her angrier than a bully.

Star removed a paper from her pocket and punched in the number for the power company. She was listening to the automated menu when Ron O'Brien joined Cade. She heard Cade explain to his younger brother that she had no power. After that she lost track of their conversation as she had one of her own with the power company. When she ended her call, both brothers were gone and she was alone.

Star knew she should make her escape, but she couldn't resist looking around the foyer. As a young girl, raised in low-rent apartments and Patsy's double-wide mobile home, she'd always dreamed of living in a real house.

To Star's surprise, the O'Brien place looked the same and still smelled of freshly baked bread. Her stomach rumbled at the thought of Patsy's homemade cinnamon rolls. She'd loved to watch Patsy bake the rolls for the B & B guests. Patsy always brought the leftover rolls home for Star and her sisters. Star had savored each bite of those cinnamon rolls, making them last as long as she possibly could. Homemade treats weren't found in the White household. Her mother's culinary skills stopped at Kraft Macaroni and Cheese.

She'd always been fascinated with the O'Brien house, especially the architecture. The big Victorian had all the charm of its time period: the wrap around porch, the gabled roof, the well-crafted built-ins, and from what she could see so far, the O'Briens hadn't done much updating. Star suppressed a grin. Maybe she'd offer her services. This was just the kind of house her boss loved to feature on *Update This!*

She glanced down at the mahogany floor, imagining how the wood would look refinished. The area rug was new, and she suspected they went through at least one rug a year here. No carpet could survive the winter snow and spring mud for more than one season.

A pretty young woman came down the hall toward her, wiping her hands on her apron, the apron covering a very large, pregnant belly.

"Hello," she said, smiling. "Can I help you?"

"I was using the phone," Star said. "Cade let me in. I'm Star White from next door."

"Star White?" The woman's mouth turned up into a wide smile. "I'm Trudy." She extended her hand and Star took it. "Do you remember me?"

"Trudy Ramsey, right?" Star asked. Trudy had been a couple of years younger than Star, but she remembered the pretty brunette with the Snow White complexion. She'd always been welcoming when Star's family had returned to Seward.

"It's Trudy O'Brien now." She looked lovingly at Ron, who'd followed her into the foyer. "I married this handsome guy. Ron, do you remember Starlene White?"

"Hey, Star," Ron said, extending his hand. "Good to see you, although it's not a surprise. I figured you might show up after we sent the letter. I hope we didn't catch you too off-guard."

"No," Star told him. "Patsy's place needs to be dealt with. I don't know why I've put it off this long. It's just a sad time." "Of course it is," Trudy said, giving Star a sympathetic smile. "I told Ron to let the place be, but Cade is in a hurry to get the footing for the new house poured before the fall rains get here." She patted her belly. "We need the room. Ron and I intend to move into the new house once it's done. We'll have two bed and breakfast sites. O'Brien Charters is booked solid. It's an exciting time."

"Sounds like it," Star said, although she couldn't imagine living the lifestyle the O'Briens did, houseguests all the time, your paycheck depending on the fish run. No, thanks.

A little girl skipped into the room. Cade followed, a white kitten in his hands. Star was still trying to process big Cade holding the tiny kitten when the little girl stopped in front of her.

"Who are you?" the girl asked, squinting up at Star.

"I'm Star."

"Star's a pretty name," the little girl said.

"What's your name?" Star asked.

"Emma."

"Pleased to meet you, Emma." Star shook hands with the girl.

"I found a kitten." Emma turned to Cade. "She scratched me." Emma showed Star the back of her hand, pointing to the bandage covering the wound. "She didn't mean to hurt me. Daddy fixed the scratch. He's taking my kitten outside for me."

"I see." Star glanced at Cade, struggling to imagine him doctoring the little girl.

"Come on, Em," Cade said with a nod toward the door. "Let's get the kitty outside."

Emma held the door open for Cade. When they were gone, Star said, "Cade's got two kids? Wow."

"Cade's got three kids," Ron told her. "The twins, Finn and Emma, are eight. He also has a sixteen-year-old son, Brad."

"Three kids," Star said. "Imagine that." Three kids equaled a ton of work. She remembered what a handful Brandi, Tawney, and Ruby Sue had been. Kids meant responsibility, big responsibility, the biggest. She'd take her job over kids any day.

"I met Finn earlier," Star said. "He was in Patsy's trailer when I got here."

"Again?" Trudy exchanged a worried look with Ron. "I know Cade's warned him not to play over there."

"He liked Patsy," Ron said with a shrug. "She was like a grandma to the kids. Especially after their mother died. Did you know that Patsy continued to bake bread and cinnamon rolls for us until the end? We all miss her."

"Thanks for saying that," Star said, touched by the kind words. "I miss her, too."

"Of course you do," Trudy said. "There's been a lot of sadness in this house the past few years with Dan and Patsy passing on and of course Marissa."

"Marissa?" Star asked.

"Cade's wife." Trudy's eyes went all soft. "Two years ago. A car accident."

"I'm sorry," Star said, surprised to find she meant the words. Every kid needed a mother, even Cade's.

"Are you staying at Patsy's?" Trudy asked.

"If the power's on when I get back over there. I just called the power company. They assured me the power should be on soon."

"But what if it's not?" Trudy asked. "Stay for dinner."

"Oh, no," Star said a bit too quickly. "I don't want to impose."

"Don't be silly," Trudy said. "You don't have power. In fact, you could stay here tonight. We have one room open."

"It's the start of our busy season," Ron said. "We have a full house starting tomorrow. Take the room, Star."

"Stay for dinner," Trudy said again.

The screen opened and Cade joined them.

"We've invited Star for dinner," Trudy said. "Don't you

think that's a great idea, Cade? It would give us all a chance to catch up."

"Sure," Cade said, but Star didn't believe him. Wariness shadowed his eyes, as if he didn't trust her. Well, he didn't need to worry. She had no intention of sharing a meal with Cade and his family. She wasn't good enough to eat with them when she'd been a kid, so why change things now?

"Thanks for the invite, but I planned on packing tonight," Star said. "I don't have a lot of time. I'm here on business, and my time to work on the trailer is limited."

"I insist you eat dinner with us." Trudy placed her hands on her hips. "It's been so long since I've had another woman to talk to. Just looking at your shoes makes me drool. I'm starved for a conversation on fashion. Please stay."

Star thought of the groceries she'd bought in town, of the cold salad she'd probably have.

"I'm making homemade chicken potpie," Trudy coaxed.

Star's mouth watered at the thought of chicken potpie. She never ate that many calories at a time and couldn't remember the last time she'd eaten anything homemade.

Star took a step toward the door. "No, I should go."

Trudy's face fell. "Are you sure I can't change your mind?" Disappointment oozed from her words.

"Some other time?" Star asked. "I really do want to get settled."

"Why don't you run Star home, Cade?" Ron suggested, giving his brother a pointed look.

"That's okay," Star said quickly. "I can walk." She didn't want to be alone in a vehicle with Cade, even if the drive was short. The man set her on edge. She didn't trust him, didn't like him.

Cade pointed at her feet. "In those shoes?"

"Cade's right," Trudy said. "Save your shoes. If you won't stay for dinner, at least take the ride."

"No, I'm fine." Star went to the door. "Thanks for the use of your phone. I really appreciate it."

On her way across the yard, she spied Finn playing with

14

Emma. The two looked nothing alike. Finn had Cade's black hair, while Emma's hair was a beautiful shade of red. Both twins sat on the grass, petting the kitten.

Star waved as she passed.

The minute she hit the trail, her feet began to ache, so much, she almost wished she'd taken the ride from Cade.

Almost.

CHAPTER TWO

Star pulled her hair up into a ponytail. She slid her feet into her comfy yellow flip-flops, noting the blisters on her heels. While the walk back from the O'Brien house may have saved her pride, her feet were now paying the price, but it was a small price to pay when it came to taking nothing from Cade O'Brien.

Ready to work, Star glanced around, wondering where she should start. With Patsy's room? The bedroom was sure to be full of memories. Maybe she'd wait until tomorrow to tackle that room with Brandi.

Star did a quick check on the second bedroom. The room was crammed full of Patsy's art supplies and canvases—too many to weed through when she was this tired, although she did look forward to going through her aunt's paintings. Patsy's paintings were the biggest reason she'd decided to close out the house herself. She couldn't bear to see them thrown away or destroyed. Her aunt lived on those canvases. Star hoped to find one or two paintings to take home with her, and she felt certain her sisters would like mementos as well.

Star turned her attention to the kitchen. She paused in front of the refrigerator. Stuck to the fridge with a magnet shaped like a whale, was a faded photo of Star, Ruby Sue,

Tawney, and Brandi.

Star's heart broke for the little girls they'd been. The photo had been taken on their first day with Patsy. Star had just turned ten. A little mother already, she held a baby Brandi in her arms with Ruby Sue and Tawney sitting on either side of her. Newly abandoned by their mother, Star could see the fear in her eyes, the desperation. All four girls looked dirty, unkempt, and miserable.

Sadness filled Star's chest. She removed the photo, tossing it into an empty box on the counter.

As Star worked to pack up Patsy's life, she remembered her aunt in the kitchen, flipping pancakes, making Star a special malted milk, and wiping her face with a wet dishrag. Good memories. Patsy, the ultimate caregiver.

When they'd been here, life had a routine. They had bedtimes, regular meals, and clean clothes to wear. They were never late for school. Their homework was done. And best of all, Star didn't have to be the mother. Sometimes it had been hard to give up that control. Star smiled. She'd gotten into it with Patsy more than once over parenting issues.

"Miss you, Pats," Star said, wishing she'd had the chance to say goodbye. Star's heart broke all over again when she thought of Patsy dying here alone. No one should have to die alone. Star prayed the heart attack had been swift, Patsy's suffering minimal.

The hum of a vehicle coming up the drive pulled Star from the box of Tupperware she loaded. She peered out the broken front window, recognizing the O'Brien truck.

Cade.

And he had Finn with him.

Star tensed. Old habits died hard. What did Cade want? After her earlier trip down memory lane, she didn't know how much more she could take today. She met Cade and Finn at the door, feeling more like she was preparing for battle than greeting neighbors.

"Hi, Star," Finn called on his way up the steps, Cade right behind him.

"What brings you two here?" she asked with wary curiosity.

"We brought you dinner," Finn said, and Star noticed the foil-covered dish in Cade's hands.

"Trudy insisted," Cade said.

"How thoughtful," Star replied, warmed by Trudy's gesture.

Cade had obviously showered, changing into clean jeans and black T-shirt with *O'Brien Charters* written in neat script across his chest. Star couldn't help but remember what he looked like under that T-shirt, all hard muscle and tanned skin. So good looking. Such a jerk.

"We were hoping the chicken potpie could act as a peace offering for Finn being in the house when you arrived," Cade told her. "I hope he didn't scare you."

"Just a little." Star smiled. Heaven help her, she could smell the chicken potpie and her stomach responded. She took the casserole dish from Cade, the ceramic still warm in her hands. "Thanks. Come over any time, Finn, if it means I get a home cooked meal."

Finn smiled, revealing a missing front tooth.

"He won't be bothering you again." Cade leveled a stern look on his son. "Right, Finn?"

"But Star said I could come over." Finn's lower lip jutted out.

"With your dad's permission," Star said the words leaving her mouth before she could stop them. No matter how much she disliked Cade, she didn't want to mess with the way he parented.

"Can I bring Emma?" Finn asked.

"Sure."

"And Snowbell?" Finn said.

"Snowbell?" Star asked.

"Our kitten," Finn told her proudly.

"Ah," Star said. "Sure, bring her over. I love kittens. I always wanted a cat but was never allowed to have one. We never stayed any place long enough to have a pet."

Star stole a look at Cade. His mouth had tightened into a frown, and she wondered what he had to frown about. In her eyes, he'd had it all when they'd been kids, parents who loved and cared for him, a big, beautiful house, money. Did he even appreciate any of it? He'd been born lucky, while she'd had to scratch and claw her way out of dysfunction and poverty.

"We should be going." Cade placed a hand on Finn's shoulder. "Come on, Finn."

"Bye, Star," Finn said before turning to follow his dad.

"Get in the truck," Cade said to his son.

Finn did as his father asked, then Cade wheeled around walking back to her.

Again, Star braced herself, for what? A confrontation? A mean remark? Ridiculous. They were adults now.

"I owe you an apology," Cade said from the base of the porch steps, those blue eyes of his glittering. "It's not you, Star. It's never been you."

Before Star could process the words, he turned and climbed into the truck, revving the engine loudly before reversing down the drive.

Cade O'Brien had just given her a backhanded apology.

Why?

It was a full minute before Star remembered the casserole dish warming her hands—the peace offering. Had he laced the food with poison? Did she dare eat it? Star shook her head.

She was being ridiculous. She was going to eat the chicken potpie, and she was going to enjoy every single bite.

Cade O'Brien be damned.

* * *

Star woke with a start.

At first she couldn't remember where she was, but thanks to the seventeen plus hours of daylight Seward enjoyed this time of year, she quickly got her bearings. She didn't move, didn't breathe. Something had woken her, but what?

She strained her ears, listening.

"Give me a beer," a young male voice said from outside Star's bedroom window.

Star bolted out of bed and went to the closet, to Patsy's gun. She'd located the pistol before going to bed, not wanting to be caught unaware if confronted by an animal or something worse. Star reached for the hatbox. In her haste, she dropped the box, the clatter alarmingly loud. She froze.

"What was that?" a second voice asked.

Star's heart hammered so loud she was sure the boys could hear it.

"Shhh," someone else said.

"Something's in there."

"Come on, let's go see."

They were coming in. Star ripped the lid from the box, her fingers closing over the gun. She didn't grab the bullets out of her aunt's boot, knowing she could never shoot anyone. Instead, she prayed the sight of the gun would frighten the boys away if it seemed like things were getting out of hand.

What had she been thinking, staying here alone? The O'Briens were close, but not so close they'd hear her scream if she were attacked. Her hands shook as she held the gun. On silent feet, she walked to the bedroom window. The boys stood in a group. One of them dropped a beer can to the ground and crushed it with his foot.

Had Patsy's place become a hangout for teenagers? They were on the back side of the mobile home. Maybe they hadn't seen her car, maybe they didn't even know she was there. Maybe she was overreacting.

Star left the bedroom. At the front door she flipped on the outdoor lights, praying they'd notice the lights, even though it was light outside.

"What the—" one of the kids said.

"Someone *is* in there."

"I'm outta here," one of the boys said.

Star edged closer to the kitchen window and sneaked a peek. One of the boys looked right at her, a boy with Cade O'Brien's face. Holy cow. The guy had one dominant gene pool.

"Hey, it's a chick," one of the boys said.

"Let's go," the boy with Cade's face replied.

Star watched as they left the clearing. She counted five teenaged boys as they disappeared into the woods. Once they were gone, the tension began to ease from Star's body. They were kids, for goodness sake. Kids.

Star set the gun on the kitchen counter. Get a grip, she told herself. One of the boys was obviously Cade's son. But why was he out here in the middle of the night? Did Cade even know where the kid was? Should she tell him?

Star poured herself a drink of water, forcing the cool liquid down her throat. It wasn't enough. She needed something stronger to steady her nerves and she wondered if Patsy still kept a bottle of brandy. Star rifled through the pantry, finding the bottle on the top shelf, way in the back. Dust coated the bottle. Star ran it under the tap before twisting the lid off. She poured an inch of brandy in a glass and gulped the amber liquid, coughing as the brandy burned its way through her body, warming her toes.

Slowly, her mind cleared.

The boys were gone, but would they be back? As much as she hated seeing Cade again, telling him about his son was probably the best option. She didn't want another late night visit. If Cade knew, he was sure to keep a better eye on his son. It seemed his kids ran wild. First Finn, now this older boy. Tomorrow she'd take his casserole dish back and talk to him. She'd want to know if it were her kid running around in the middle of the night.

Star was about to turn out the light and head back to bed when a noise on the front porch startled her. Her eyes darted to the gun the same instant a knock sounded at the door.

Her adrenal glands kicked into overdrive. Had one of the boys come back? She wasn't cut out for this much late night drama.

"I have a gun," she called out, "and I know how use it."

"What the heck? Star?" Cade's voice said from the other

side of the door.

"O'Brien?" She didn't know whether to be relieved or irritated.

"What's going on?" The doorknob rattled. "Open the door."

Star crossed the room and unlocked the door. If his tone was any indication of his mood, he'd probably kick the door down if she didn't let him in.

Cade stood on the porch, dressed in gray sweats and the same T-shirt he'd worn earlier. His black hair stuck up, as if he'd rolled from bed, run his fingers through it, and hurried over to her place.

"What're you doing here?" she asked definitely irritated now. "Doesn't anybody sleep in this town?"

"What're you doing with a gun?" he countered, pushing his way past her. He glanced around, located the gun, and picked it up. "Are you crazy? This thing is real. Do you even know how to use a gun?"

"Relax, it's not loaded." She snatched the weapon from him. "See?" She opened the chamber, giving him a full view of the empty chambers. "Besides, I wouldn't have needed a gun at all if you kept your kid inside at night."

Cade frowned. "Brad was here?"

"He looks just like you. Brad was here, along with four other boys. They woke me up. They were out back, drinking beer."

Cade shook his head. "I heard Brad sneak out, but I didn't see which way he went. I figured he might head this way. It's not the first time he's come here. It's one of the reasons I want to mow this place down and build the new B & B. This place has become a gathering place for teenagers."

"What are the other reasons?" Star couldn't resist asking, sure he wanted to erase her family from his memory.

"What are you getting at, Star?" Cade asked, his tone deadly soft.

Her back stiffened. "Admit it, you've never liked us, or more specifically, me."

The muscle in his jaw jumped. "I had issues."

"Issues?" Star picked up her glass of brandy.

"Mind if I have a drink?" Cade asked, the question catching her off guard.

"Suit yourself." Star slid the bottle to him, along with a glass.

Cade splashed the liquid into the glass and downed the brandy in a single gulp.

"That kid's going to be the death of me." Cade grimaced as the liquor worked its way through his body.

For a second, Star could see Cade's pain, feel his upset over his son's behavior. Heaven help her, he almost seemed human. Almost.

"Raising kids is tough," she offered. "Believe me, I know."

"How do you know, Star?" Cade asked. "Do you have kids?"

"Absolutely not," she said, "and I never will. I raised my three sisters. That was enough for me."

Cade stared at her, as if he were trying to figure her out. "It's not the same."

"It is for me," Star said. "I've been through the teenage rebellion with my sisters. I remember those years. The drinking. The sneaking out. The calls from the police. Been there, done that, not doing it again."

"Brad is sixteen," Cade said. "Too young to be drinking."

"Really?" Star asked, amused. "I seem to remember you indulging once or twice around that age. As I recall, beer made you even meaner." There, she'd thrown the truth at him. Would he crush her with horrible words? Would he deny he'd been mean to her?

"I deserved that," he said, the words tired. "I was a mixed up kid who'd lost his mother. I took out my pain on you. I know it's not an excuse, but it's all I've got. We're both adults now, adults with adult problems. Can we let the past go?"

"Just like that?" She stared at him, looking for the boy he used to be, but she didn't see the mean boy from her childhood, instead she saw a man, a man with an awful lot on his plate.

"I need to go." He set his glass on the counter, glaring at it as if it had held poison instead of liquor. "Thanks for the drink, and I'll make sure that Brad and his friends don't bother you again."

At the door, he turned. "If you do find the need to shoot that gun, do us both a favor and aim it toward the sky. I'll hear the shot and be here in minutes. Don't take aim at anything on the ground. The place is crawling with kids and pets."

From the window, Star watched Cade go, a different Cade, a more mature Cade. He'd been an angry kid, but she hadn't realized he'd been acting out of grief. And while Cade's grief didn't excuse his bad behavior, Star did feel some compassion toward him now. Maybe his childhood hadn't been as perfect as she'd imagined. Maybe they had more in common than she thought. Cade was raising his kids alone. All those motherless kids.

Star understood better than most how draining a houseful of kids could be. She'd been babysitting her sisters before she'd reached the double-digits. She'd taken over their care completely at age sixteen when her mother had disappeared with husband number four. Somehow, she'd held things together, getting the girls off to school, fixing them meals, putting them to bed while keeping her own grades up and working a part-time job.

She probably could have kept her mother's disappearance a secret longer, but bills had come due. Not knowing what else to do, Star had called Patsy. Patsy had flown to Vegas, packed them up and taken them to Seward—their home away from home. It was a pattern they'd repeated over and over during Star's childhood.

She'd never understood why her mother had had so many children; Star only knew she'd never have kids of her own. She couldn't do it again. She had nothing left to give.

That's why she was a single, city girl, and she always would be.

CHAPTER THREE

"Hurry up, Dad," Brad said, one foot on the dock, the other on the boat. "I need to get home."

"What's the rush?" Cade took a minute to enjoy the view of the bay, of the blue-gray water and the azure sky dotted with white clouds. Sometimes he just needed a hit of the beauty. Instantly revived and in a better frame of mind to deal with Brad, he said, "We're not done here. Get back on the boat."

They'd just docked and had a good thirty minutes of work ahead of them before they made their way home. Trudy had picked their guests up in the van a few minutes ago, taking them back to the house so they could clean up. Brad knew the routine. They had to close up the boat and deal with the fish before they'd join the paying guests back at the house.

Cade glanced at Brad. The kid wore his trademark frown.

"The faster you work, the faster you get to go home," Cade said.

Brad turned on the pump and quickly worked to scour the fish box.

"You're grounded, remember?" Cade reminded him.

For a second, Brad looked like he wanted to turn the hose on Cade, but just as quickly the kid erased the hostility from his features. Cade turned away, biting back a smile. No matter how mad Brad was, he'd never openly defy Cade. Deep down Brad was a good kid. They were just going through a rough patch, growing pains. Brad was well on his way to becoming a man, whether Cade liked it or not.

The water shut off. Cade secured the cabin. He wiped down the table, and disposed of the last of the garbage. Done, he left the cabin, locking the door behind him.

He turned in time to see Brad put the plug back in the fish box. The kid snapped the lid closed, then straightened, before wiping his hands on his jeans. Cade oiled the fishing poles while Brad swabbed the deck, and then put away a stray life vest.

"Ready?" Cade asked when the boat was tidy.

"Yep," Brad replied.

Cade stepped off the *Mary Rose* first, Brad behind him. Water lapped at the pier, the sound as soothing as the motion of the dock under his rubber boots. Cade inhaled, the salt air going deep into his lungs, salt air mixed with the smell of fish guts. Man, he loved that smell. To this day the scents stoked him, reminding him of warm summers and the days of endless free-time and fishing just for the pure joy of the sport.

Cade grabbed one handle of the cooler that held the day's catch, Brad automatically took the other. They walked up the gangplank toward the parking lot.

"Good day, Cade?" Cy Alder called as they passed by. The retired fisherman spent his afternoons sitting on the same bench, asking the same question of each local fisherman as they stepped off the pier each day.

"The boat limited." Cade grinned. They hefted the cooler of fish up into the bed of the truck. "No kings, but some impressive silvers."

Cy nodded. "Good day then."

"Yep," Cade agreed. He liked it when the boat limited, when all the customers were happy. Happy customers meant repeat business.

Brad climbed into the truck, in the driver's seat.

26

Cade was trying to decide if he wanted to pick a fight with Brad and tell the kid to slide over when he spied Star and Brandi coming out of Finnegan's Restaurant. The two women chatted away. Brandi's hand rested on her huge belly. When was she going to have that baby anyway? It seemed like she'd been pregnant forever. He couldn't help but notice the difference between the two sisters. They looked nothing alike, and why would they? They didn't share the same father. Brandi had dark brown curly hair and brown eyes. And while Brandi was pretty, Star was a show-stopper, a real looker just like her mom.

Brad honked the horn to get Cade's attention.

Both Star and Brandi looked right at him.

"Hey, Cade." Brandi waved. She took Star's arm, practically dragging her across the street.

Cade went to the driver's door of the truck, yanking it open. "Slide over." The honking of the horn had doubled his irritation with Brad.

"I want to drive," Brad whined. "What good's a license if I never get to use it?"

"I said, slide over. Driving is a privilege, one you have to earn. After last night, I'm not sure when driving is going to be part of your life again."

"Cade," Brandi said, forcing him to acknowledge the sisters.

He turned and noted that Star looked about as happy as he did at the forced meeting. "Ladies."

"Any chance you could give Star a lift home?" Brandi asked, the words coming out in the rush.

His gaze cut to Star.

"It's really not necessary." Star shot her sister the "death" look. "I can drop you off, Brandi, and take your car."

"But he's going your way." Brandi turned her doe eyes on Cade. "You'd be doing me a favor. Sally called in sick and I can get an extra shift at the diner if I can get over there ASAP."

"Brandi—" Star started to protest.

"Hop in," Cade said, cutting her off. "It's no problem."

"Are you sure?" Star's brow wrinkled as if she were unconvinced.

"Positive." Cade leaned into the truck. "Jump in the back, Brad."

Brad sighed, loudly and rudely, before he got out of the truck and into the rear seat.

"Thank you, Cade," Brandi said. To Star she said, "Bye." The two sisters hugged. "I know we didn't get as much done today as we wanted, but I'll get back over tomorrow. Then we'll tackle Patsy's room. I promise."

"Only if you're up to it," Star said. "You need to rest. You don't need to be working extra shifts."

"We need the money." Brandi patted her belly. "Babies aren't cheap."

Cade walked around the truck and opened the passenger door for Star.

Star finally separated from her sister. "Thanks," she said as she climbed into the truck.

Cade closed her door. A minute later they pulled out.

"I don't think you've officially met Brad," Cade said, giving a head nod toward the back seat. "Brad, this is Star White, the woman you nearly scared to death last night."

Star twisted around. "Hi, Brad." She extended her hand.

Cade glanced in the rearview mirror, watching as his son shook her hand.

"Sorry about last night," Brad said, the words clipped and forced—expected. "We didn't know anyone was there."

"No harm done," Star said in a business-like tone. She twisted back around, but Cade didn't miss the way Brad's eyes roved over Star. The kid thought Star was hot.

Cade stole a glance at her. *She was hot.* Her long legs were poured into dark denim jeans, and like yesterday, her strappy black sandals had absurdly high heels. Wasn't there a lewd name for shoes like those? The shoes were totally inappropriate for a town where people lived in boots much of the year. A soft pink T-shirt hugged her breasts. She'd always had great curves in all the right places. And nice legs. His body tightened. His hands clenched the steering wheel. Man, he couldn't control his own reaction to her. No wonder his kid looked all love sick.

"Catch many fish today?" Star turned her pretty green eyes on Cade, and he instantly remembered every mean thing he'd ever done to her. Even now he didn't fully understand how things had spiraled so out of control between them. When he looked at her now, the last thing he wanted to do was hurt or embarrass her. Despite how he'd treated her, Star had managed to shake off her awful childhood and rise above it. She didn't belong here, she never had. And maybe that was one of the reasons he'd given her such a hard time. Even dirt poor, with a family so lousy you couldn't have made them up, she'd always held her head high, always letting him know that she was as good as he was, better than he was. He knew it. She knew it. End of story.

"The boat limited," he said, forcing the past from his mind. "This is our busy time of year."

"I remember," she said almost wistfully.

"We need to make a quick stop at Logan's to drop off the fish," Cade said.

"Logan's," Star said. "They do the packaging for you, right?"

"Right. How many summers did you spend here?" Cade asked, wondering if her memories of her time spent here were as vivid as his.

"Four, maybe five?" She sounded uncertain. "I'm not sure. We came and went from here so many times. I do remember I turned seventeen that last summer. The following summer I started college at the University of Washington. That much I remember."

His mouth went dry. "I remember, too." He remembered how she'd driven him crazy in her short shorts and halter tops. By then, she was totally off limits. He'd already met Marissa, already gotten her pregnant and was headed down the aisle.

"You were home from college that last summer. You worked on the boat." Star turned to Brad. "Looks like you're following in your dad's footsteps."

"I guess," Brad said sullenly.

"It's nice you have a family business," Star said with obvious envy. "The closest thing I've got to a family business is a mother who deals blackjack and a sister who's a Vegas showgirl."

"You have a sister who's a showgirl?" Brad asked, suddenly interested in the conversation. "Cool."

Cade exchanged an amused look with Star.

"What do you do, Star?" Cade asked, curious about the woman Star had become.

"I'm the production manager for *Update This!*" she said with obvious pride. "Have you heard of it?"

"Nope."

"It's a cable show. We take a room in an older house and update it. You should tune in sometime."

"I don't watch much TV," Cade said, almost wishing he did. He wanted to find some kind of common ground with her, some way to bridge the gap he'd created between them.

Star gave him a tight smile. "Believe it or not, O'Brien, there's a great, big world out there that doesn't revolve around fish."

"Do you know any movie stars?" Brad asked.

"Some. From time to time we feature celebrity homes on *Update This!* Oh, hey, I met Katy Perry once. My boss got me backstage passes and I took my sister to her concert in Vegas."

"She's hot," Brad said.

Star's hand slid down her thigh. "I guess she is."

Cade's gut tightened. How many times had Star filled his teenage fantasies? Too many to count. He put his focus back on the road.

"So you're from Vegas?" Brad asked.

"Not really. I split my time between Vegas and Seward when I was a kid. I live in Seattle now. *Update This!* is filmed in Seattle."

"I've been to Seattle," Brad said. "I've been to the top of the Space Needle."

"I worked there when I was in college," Star told him. "I was a photographer."

"Cool," Brad said.

"Brad's looking at applying to the University of Washington," Cade interjected.

"You should," Star said to Brad. "It's a great school. Lots of fun, too."

"I'll bet the parties are awesome." Brad had really perked up now, his obvious enthusiasm for anything Star said starting to annoy Cade.

Star shrugged. "I wasn't much of a party girl."

Cade found that hard to believe. She was her mother's daughter after all.

When they reached Logan's, Cade and Brad quickly offloaded the fish. Back in the truck, Brad and Star continued to chat until Cade pulled the truck into Star's driveway.

Star reached down to retrieve her purse, and Cade caught another whiff of her light, clean, citrus scent. Again, his gut tightened. She straightened, set the purse on her lap, then opened the truck door. Before she exited, she turned to Brad. "Nice to meet you."

"Same here," Brad said, giving Star a head nod.

"Thanks for the lift, O'Brien."

"Anytime."

Star smiled, but her smile didn't reach her eyes. She still hated him, and he didn't blame her.

But that didn't stop Cade from watching her walk in those ridiculously high heels to the mobile home. How did she do it? Those shoes had to be four or five inches high. She was a city girl all right. Beautiful and expensive.

"Dad?"

"What?"

"Can we go now?"

Giving himself a mental shake, Cade put the truck into

reverse and backed down the driveway.

.

CHAPTER FOUR

The following morning, Star rose early, eager to get a jump on her day. As usual, when she thought about work, a fire lit inside her. She loved her job, loved going to work every day, even when her work did take her to her hometown.

Due at ten to meet with her Seward, Alaska man, Evan Jenson, Star jogged four miles by 8:30, hit the shower by 8:35, and was just adding silver hoop earrings to her outfit, a pearl gray tie-front short-sleeved jacket with matching slacks, when she heard a car outside.

Barefoot, she padded to the door, surprised to see Cade's truck rolling to a stop. Why wasn't he out fishing? A sixth sense told her something was wrong. They hadn't exactly parted on good terms yesterday. He still rubbed her the wrong way. She hated the way he looked at her, as if she were good enough to take to bed, but not good enough to meet his parents.

Star stepped out onto the porch. "Hey," she called when he exited the truck. "What's up?"

Cade walked toward her, well, swaggered was more like it. His lazy stare slid down her body to her bare feet before rising again to her eyes, his perusal upping her agitation. She resisted the urge to ask him if he liked what he saw.

"We had a call at our place this morning," he said in a way

that put her on red alert.

"What kind of call?" Star asked. "Is it Brandi?"

He nodded, confirming her worst fear. "She's at Providence. Bud said something about possible toxemia. He wants you to come."

"Oh, no." Star went back inside and quickly located the gray sling back heels that matched her suit. Once the shoes were on her feet, she snagged her matching purse from the bed and met Cade in the kitchen.

His eyebrows shot up when he saw her. "You're dressed pretty fancy for a day of packing."

"I have to work today," she said. "Evan's expecting me. I have to call him. Does your cell phone work here?"

"Nope, not until we're about two miles out of town," Cade said. "Are you talking about Evan Jenson?"

"Do you know him?" They stepped outside and Star pulled the door closed.

"There's only one Evan in town. What do you want with him?"

"He's my Alaska man for the Seward show." Star opened the passenger door on her rental car and tossed her purse inside. "*Update This!* is remodeling his kitchen and bedroom and trying to fix him up with a date."

"What?" Cade asked, as if he couldn't believe what he was hearing.

"Look," Star said, losing patience. "I need to go." She started around the car to the driver's side, but Cade caught her arm.

"Let me drive you, Star."

His touch was gentle, his tone gentler still, but that didn't stop Star from pulling her arm free. "No, thanks."

"You're upset. I'll drive you to Providence. It's the least I can do."

He took the keys from her and Star was instantly reminded of the time he'd taken her lunch from her on the school bus and proceeded to play keep away with Ron. He'd made her cry. Well, not this time.

"I'll drive myself," she said stiffly. "I'm fine." Star reached for her keys, but he slid them into the front pocket of his jeans. As if she'd ever go after them there. "Look, I need my car. I told you, I have to work today. Give me the keys."

"Nope." He went to the driver's side. "Let's go. I'll drive your car. Trudy can pick me up."

"You're being a bully. I don't need your help," Star said, more annoyed with him than she'd ever been. "I can take care of my sister, O'Brien. I've been doing it for years."

"But who takes care of you, Star?"

The kindness in his tone threw her, made her wonder what his game was. "I take care of myself." They faced each other, the open car door sandwiched between them. "Please give me the keys."

His eyes searched her face but instead of seeing meanness or hate like the old days, she saw compassion and tenderness. Those emotions made her feel too much. Star refused to acknowledge the vulnerability rising inside her. She hated that Cade knew so much about her dysfunctional family, hated the long forgotten pain stirring inside her. He made her feel ten years old, beaten down by a life she couldn't control.

"Get in the car," he said. "Let me take care of you."

"Why?" she asked, at her wit's end.

"Because I want to. I owe you." Cade glanced away from her, then back. "You know I do."

They'd reached a stalemate of sorts. Star knew Cade wouldn't back down, he never did. The need to see Brandi outweighed her desire to argue with him. Star got in the car. A minute later they were on the road to town.

Silently, she contemplated calling the police as soon as her phone had service but to report what? Cade giving her a ride to see her sister? Even to her that sounded ridiculous. More than anything she wanted to give him the silent treatment but too many questions bounced around in her head.

"What else did Bud say?" she asked.

"Just that she started feeling sick last night. Swelling. First thing this morning, he took her to the doctor."

35

"I hope the baby's okay." Star pressed her hands together. Didn't babies die from toxemia? Brandi wanted this baby so much. She couldn't bear to think of her sister suffering the loss of a child. "I can't stand not having phone service."

"She'll be okay."

Star glanced at Cade. He looked away from the road briefly, making eye contact with her. Again, she saw the foreign kindness, yet she couldn't let go, couldn't accept anything good from him yet.

"Why aren't you fishing?" Star asked. "You have all those guests."

"Ron took the boat out this morning. The boat only needs one skipper. We trade off."

When they reached the medical center, Cade cut the engine and passed Star her keys.

"Let me know if I can do anything else to help," he said.

Star took the keys from him. "Thank you."

Star went straight to the information desk and was given directions to where Brandi was. She entered the room to find her sister pale, her forehead creased with worry, her hands resting protectively over her large belly, as if sheer will would keep the baby safe inside her. Star's worry meter spiked. Brandi's eyes, wide with fear, fixed on Star.

"Hey," Star said softly.

"Star," Brandi cried, relief sagging her shoulders. "Oh, Star."

Brandi's husband, Bud, rose from his chair next to the bed. "Star. Thanks for coming."

Star had always liked Bud. He was an honest, what-you-see-is-what-you-get kind of guy. His sandy blond hair was mussed, as if he'd been wearing a hat but had discarded it. He was dressed in his work uniform, navy pants and work shirt, his name embroidered on the right pocket below the words Sherman Electric.

Star grasped Bud's hand on her way by. "How are things going here?"

"Better," Bud replied, but she heard the worry in his tone,

and to her he looked older than his twenty-two years.

Large tears filled Brandi's eyes, spilling over onto her pale cheeks. "I'm scared, Star. They want to move me to Anchorage, to the hospital there. They want to do a C-section."

"Women have C-sections every day." Star sat on the edge of the bed and smoothed Brandi's curls from her forehead. "Everything will be fine. Women get toxemia all the time."

"I know." Brandi rubbed her belly. "I thought the swelling was from being on my feet all day at the diner. I didn't realize it was more serious. If anything happens to my baby..."

"Nothing's going to happen," Star assured her, covering her own fears.

"At least he's moving," Brandi said. "I know he's okay."

Star smiled. "That's great." She touched Brandi's belly. Brandi's hand closed over Star's and she moved it. A tiny kick met Star's palm. "Was that him?" she asked with wonder.

"Yes."

The baby kicked Star again. "Oh, my."

Brandi smiled. "You see why I love him so much already?"

"I do." But Star didn't. She didn't understand at all why someone would want to feel that responsible for another human life. She remembered how scared she'd been when the girls had been sick or injured, how helpless she'd felt to make them well. She'd even stolen a bottle of cough syrup once when Brandi had been ill. She'd been so desperate to make her sister better.

A knock sounded on the door. Before anyone entered, Bud opened the door and then disappeared into the hall.

"Cade's here," Star said at Brandi's concerned look. "That was probably him. He insisted on driving me."

"*Really?*" Brandi asked.

"He strong-armed me."

"He's taking care of you," Brandi said in a knowing tone. "Just like you're taking care of me. I always thought he had a crush on you. He just had a funny way of showing it. He's a good guy, Star. Give him a chance."

"Don't get melodramatic, Brandi," Star said dryly. "Don't confuse a need for control with kindness. And I don't care how good a guy he is, don't even think of trying to force a love connection between the two of us. There's no way I'm dating anyone from this town. Plus, I have a no-kid policy, remember? I can't even imagine letting kids loose in my condo. All those sticky fingers. Yuck."

"A no-kid policy is a dumb rule," Brandi said. "No one would make a better mother than you."

Star stuck out her tongue.

Brandi squeezed Star's fingers. "I'm glad you're here."

"Have you called Mom?" Star asked.

"No." Brandi frowned. "What's the point?"

"I'll call her," Star said. "She'll want to know."

"You can call, but you know she won't come." Brandi's hand tightened around Star's. "I need you, Star. Not her."

Star agreed. Their mother would be worthless here. She didn't know how to give comfort. That had been Star's job. "I'm going to call her anyway. Tawney and Ruby Sue, too."

Brandi nodded, and Star didn't miss the relief on her face. "Thanks."

Star rose. "Thank goodness my phone works here. You can't imagine the withdrawal I'm going through at Patsy's." Star headed for the door. "I'll be right outside. I'll send Buddy back in."

"Thanks, Star. I feel so much better just having you here. I'm so glad you're in town. I need you so much."

"I'm here as long as you need me," Star said, the words escaping before she could stop them.

"Really?" Brandi smiled, and it were as if a dark cloud had lifted. Star hadn't realized how much it meant to Brandi to have her here, how scared she really was.

"Really," Star said. "Don't you worry, Bran. I'm going to take care of everything."

"I know you will, Star," Brandi said, the words confident. "You're the best."

* * *

Cade let himself into the house and tossed his keys on the table in the foyer. What a day. After running Star to the Providence that morning, he'd come home to find a problem with the engine on the *Mary Rose*. He'd spent the rest of the day working on the boat's engine.

A soft beam of light came from the kitchen where he assumed their guests, three men from Seattle, were gathered, guests who would receive a refund for the canceled fishing trip today. Right now Cade wanted nothing more than a hot meal and a shower to wash the engine grease from his skin, but those things could wait until he checked in with Ron and their guests.

Cade started for the kitchen but took a detour when he heard the sound of canned laugher coming from the television in the family room.

Brad lay sprawled across the brown leather sofa, a can of soda on the coffee table in front of him.

"Hey," Cade said from the doorway.

Brad pulled his attention from the television to glance at Cade. The kid was barely speaking to him, still angry at Cade for grounding him.

"It looks like Star could use some help at Patsy's place," Cade said. "Her sister's in the hospital. Are you interested in lending a hand if she needs it?"

Brad focused back on the TV. "Not really."

Cade shook his head in disgust. How did he get through to Brad? He longed for the days when Brad had looked up to him and had hung on his every word. Marissa's death had changed everything between them. He understood Brad's anger, and had spent thousands of dollars on counseling hoping to mend his broken family, but he had a feeling that time and a maturity only age could bring would be what ended the rift between him and Brad.

Changing the subject, Cade asked, "Did I miss anything around here?"

Brad smirked. "Just Uncle Ron kissing the guests' butts."

Cade frowned. "Get to bed at a decent time tonight."

Brad used the remote to turn the volume up.

Cade opened his mouth to tell him to turn the sound down but decided against it. Brad was spoiling for a fight, but he was too tired to spar. Instead, Cade made his way to the kitchen.

"Hey, brother," Ron said. "Engine good?"

Cade forgot to answer. Star sat at the bar with the guests, Ron, and Trudy.

"Star dropped by to give us an update on Brandi," Trudy said.

"How is she?" Cade said to Star.

"Not good," Star said, her brows drawing together. "She's having a C-section tomorrow morning. Thank you for your help today. I know I was a mess this morning."

"No problem," Cade said. Man, he couldn't look away from her. And neither could their guests. All three men hung on Star's every word.

"So the engine's good?" Ron asked again.

"Tip top." Cade glanced down at his grease stained hands. "In fact, I should go up and wash this grease off."

"Your dinner's in the oven," Trudy said, heading for the stove. "I'm going to turn the oven off. The food's ready when you are."

"Great," Cade said. "Thanks."

"I should be leaving." Star slid off the barstool. "Thanks again for the tea and cookies, Trudy."

"You're welcome," Trudy said. "Stop by any time. And be sure and let us know if we can help with Brandi or with Patsy's place."

"I will." Star smiled at Trudy.

"I'll walk you out." Cade stepped forward, not willing to let her go just yet.

"Good night," Star said to the group.

A chorus of good nights followed as they left the kitchen.

Cade walked behind Star, his eyes on the sway of her hips.

What was it about her that drove him crazy with the need to get her attention?

At the door, she turned. "Good night."

"I'll walk you home," he said.

"No need." She gave him a small smile. "You're tired and I know the way by heart."

He considered arguing with her but discarded the idea. He'd already strong-armed her once today when he'd insisted on driving her to the hospital. Why he'd done that, he still didn't understand. He'd been undone by her upset, just as he'd been undone by her tears all those years ago when he'd been such a jerk to her.

"Check in with us tomorrow," Cade said.

"I will." Her lips parted.

Cade knew he stared at her mouth; he couldn't help it. She had the most beautiful mouth he'd ever seen. She frowned. He glanced away.

And then she was gone. He watched as she crossed the yard.

"You okay?" Ron asked, joining him at the door.

"Fine."

"Man." Ron ran his fingers through his hair. "I feel for Brandi and Bud. I wouldn't want to go through a C-section. The whole birth thing is scary enough the natural way."

Cade clapped his brother on the shoulder. "You won't have to."

"You and Star seem to be getting along better," Ron said. "I was worried at first. You were always such a jerk to her. I never understood why. Star and her sisters were the hottest girls, besides Trudy, in this town."

"What didn't you understand?" Cade asked. "You know why I didn't like her family."

"Dad had needs," Ron said. "Patsy filled them. If not Patsy, then he would have found someone else. End of story. You owe Star an apology."

Cade tensed. "I've already apologized."

Ron's eyebrows shot up. "Is that so? What did she say?"

"Nothing. Now butt out."

"Well, okay," Ron said, not sounding convinced.

"I'm going up to shower and check on the twins and then head to bed myself. Five a.m. is going to come early."

Ron grinned. "Your turn for the early run."

Upstairs, Cade stopped by Finn's room, listening to his son's breathing, deep and even. Cade smoothed his hair. Love for Finn filled his chest. Next he checked on Emma. The little girl slept on her side, her mouth drawn into a pucker, as if she waited for a prince to kiss her. Man, he hoped she'd find her prince one day. Someone to love and cherish her.

What the heck was wrong with him? He was going soft. Maybe he was just tired. Or maybe it was seeing Star again. She made him think about his life, about the choices he'd made.

She made him think about Marissa. Some mother he'd picked for his kids. She'd been an accident waiting to happen. And she'd almost taken his kids with her. He waited for the anger to hit him square in the chest like it always did when he thought of her, but tonight the punch wasn't as hard. She'd been gone two years now. Time had softened the rough edges of their marriage.

Cade tucked the covers more securely around Emma. With a heavy heart, he left the room, closing the door behind him.

Once in bed, he couldn't sleep. He was staring at the numbers on his alarm clock, three twenty-five a.m. when the phone rang.

Cade snatched up the phone. "Hello."

"Cade O'Brien?" a male voice asked.

"Speaking."

"This is Officer Reynolds, Seward Police."

Cade's heart lurched. "Is something wrong?"

"We've got your son in custody. He was caught up at the old water tower. He and some other boys were drinking."

"I'll be right there." Cade sat up. "Thank you for calling."

"I'll let Brad know you're on your way," the officer said.

"You do that," Cade said, his gut twisting into a hard knot. "You do that."

CHAPTER FIVE

"How far off schedule are you?" Frank Rogers asked.

Star smiled into the phone. She paced the floor of the waiting room in Anchorage Regional Hospital. Too keyed up to sit still, Star had called her boss, hoping Frank would distract her. "One day, Frank. Ease up. I'm meeting with Evan tomorrow morning; after that, I'll be back on track."

Frank sighed. "I know you need to be with your sister. I understand, I really do, but we are two weeks out from the Fairbanks shoot."

"I'll be ready," Star said to her boss. "Trust me, Frank. Have I ever let you down?"

"Okay, okay," Frank agreed. "Oh, the segment on *Bigger, Bolder, Brighter* is on track. Vivienne's in love with the project. Color is her thing."

Vivienne LaRue was the top designer on *Update This!* Of the four designers working on the show, she was a ratings favorite. Her flamboyant style and French accent gave the show sophistication and class.

"Will you ask her to call me?" Star said. "I want to talk to her about the Seward house."

"I'll pass on the message."

"Thanks. Go ahead and send me whatever you have via email."

"It's mainly the set up for the three homes on *Bigger, Bolder, Brighter*. Do what you do best, Star. Make it happen."

"I will. Now, relax, Frank. I won't let you down."

"You better not. Give your sister my best."

"Will do, Frank."

Star ended the call and stared at the double doors leading to the birthing area. What was happening? Were Brandi and the baby okay? When she'd asked for an update earlier, the desk nurse had reassured her that everything was fine. Still, Star couldn't help the anxiety that filled her. What if something went wrong? No, she refused to think that way. Brandi would be fine. The baby would be fine. Positive thoughts.

Her phone rang. Destiny's name flashed on the screen.

"Hi, Mom."

"Star?" Destiny asked in a voice that had a permanent husky note.

"It's me."

"How's Brandi? Any news yet?"

"No," Star told her. "I'm going crazy waiting."

"My poor baby," Destiny said the words dripping with sympathy. "I wish I could be there with her."

"Why don't you come, Mom?" Star asked, hoping against hope she'd say yes. "I have air miles. I could book you a ticket. My treat."

"I don't know," Destiny hedged. "I have my job."

Star could practically see her mother twirling her over-processed hair around her index finger, as if her conversation with her daughter bored her. Why couldn't Destiny be a mom for once?

"Don't you have some vacation saved up?" Star pressed, refusing to give up for Brandi's sake. Star had learned long ago to expect nothing from their mother, but Brandi's heart wasn't as hardened. Destiny's refusal to come would crush her sister.

"Some."

"Think about it. Just say the word and I'll book the ticket,"

Star said.

"I said I'll think about it, Star," her mother replied, her tone slightly defensive. "Call me when you have news."

The line went dead.

Star took a seat on a nearby chair. Her stomach churned. Darn it. She refused to let her mother get to her.

The chime of an incoming text message brought her attention to her phone.

Everything okay? Any news? Cade

Cade? She'd exchanged numbers with Cade yesterday, at his insistence, in case she needed anything, but she'd never expected him to call or text her. Should she reply? Why not?

No news yet. Star hit the send button.

Her phone chimed again. *Do you need anything?*

Aren't you working? Star texted back.

We limited early. I'm back at the house.

Before she could reply, the door leading to the birthing area swung open.

Star forgot all about Cade and came to her feet.

"Are you Star?" a woman in blue scrubs asked.

"Yes," Star said. "Is Brandi all right?"

"The doctor's with her," the nurse said. "Brandi's husband asked me to tell you that the baby's been born, a healthy boy."

Relief filled Star. "That's great."

"But there was a complication. Your sister experienced a lot of bleeding."

"What?" The bottom dropped out of Star's stomach. "Is she okay?"

The nurse nodded. "She will be. Bud has asked if you can gown-up and come in. He'd like for you to hold the baby while he sits with Brandi."

"Me?" Star said stupidly. "I'm not good with babies."

The nurse smiled. "It's easy. You'll see." The nurse started for the birthing area.

Star's phone chimed.

Cade: *Are you there?*

Quickly Star replied, *Brandi's had complications. They are asking me to come in. Gotta go.*

Star sent the message, gathered up her sweater and laptop, then followed the nurse to the birthing area.

* * *

Is this what it felt like to be hit by a truck?

Star felt drained, emotionally and physically, and she still had to make the two-hour drive back to Seward.

At least she could leave the hospital knowing that Brandi, Bud, and baby William were fine and well cared for. Brandi had stabilized. She seemed great, happy, but tired. In fact, Star had felt like an outsider for the last hour as she'd watched Brandi, Bud, and the baby snuggle together, but Brandi had insisted that Star stay until Star's stomach had rumbled so loudly, Brandi finally realized that her sister had been without food all day. At last, Brandi had given Star the go-ahead to go home.

Star headed for the elevator, eager to get back to Patsy's.

She passed through the waiting area, her focus on the elevator.

"Star."

Star halted. Cade sat in the waiting area. He unfolded himself from the chair and stood. He looked so good, so strong, and for a moment, she wanted to lean on him, wanted to let him take care of her. She didn't even want to know where that thought had come from.

"How's Brandi?" he asked, as she approached.

"She's all right now, but it was scary for a while. She had some bleeding they had trouble stopping."

"And the baby?" Cade asked.

Star smiled. "He's perfect. His name is William. Will for short. I held him for hours. I'd forgotten what it feels like to hold a newborn. Will's so tiny, so fragile. Holding him took me right back to when Brandi was born. I did more than my fair share of holding her, diapering her, feeding her."

"What? At nine or ten years old," Cade said with a shake

of his head.

Star frowned. "Destiny isn't mother material. She enjoyed getting pregnant, it was what came after that she didn't like."

Cade touched her arm. "That's rough. I'm sorry, Star."

"Don't be," Star said, rejecting his pity. She didn't even want him here. Did she? She didn't know what she wanted.

Suddenly, the day caught up with Star. She had to sit. Now.

She dropped into the nearest chair.

"Are you okay?" Cade asked, taking the seat beside her.

"It's been quite an emotional day." Star placed a hand on her rumbling stomach. "What are you doing here anyway? It's not like this place is on your way home."

"Trudy insisted. She thought you might need moral support. She would have come herself, but Ron didn't want her to make the drive."

"That was nice of Trudy," Star said. "And nice of you."

"I make the drive all the time. It's no big deal," Cade said easily. "Were you on your way out?"

"Yes."

"Trudy wanted me to invite you to dinner. She said I'm not allowed to take no for an answer. I promise we'll all be on our best behavior, especially me."

Star laughed at the pained expression on his face. "Wow, what an offer. Did Trudy make you memorize that invitation? Never mind, I don't care. I'd love to visit with Trudy and I don't feel like being alone tonight. Too much has happened today. I know I won't be able to turn my brain off. Plus, I'm starving, and I know firsthand what a good cook Trudy is."

Cade grinned at her. "You won't be sorry."

Star stood. Cade rose. He held out his hand, taking her laptop case from her. His other hand closed around her elbow, his touch gentle but firm.

Heaven help her, she was going home with Cade O'Brien. By choice. She'd definitely slipped into an alternate universe, and right now, she didn't care one bit.

CHAPTER SIX

"Oh, my gosh," Trudy said after hearing the story of Brandi's son's birth, her hands on her own pregnant belly. "I can't wait until it's my turn. She's so lucky to have her baby."

"How long do you have?" Star took a sip of her wine. They were seated around the outdoor dinner table at the O'Briens. The guests had gone into town for dinner, leaving the O'Briens to enjoy a rare night off. At the far end of the table, Emma and Finn played King's Corner. Brad had already finished eating and had gone inside, leaving the adults to their conversation and after dinner wine.

"Almost three weeks." Trudy massaged her belly. "I'm so ready to be thin again."

Star smiled. Trudy might not be svelte now but the smile on her face said it all; she had loved every minute of this pregnancy.

Across the table from Star, Cade watched her, intently. Too intently. Star glanced away, uncomfortable. Did he like her or not? She couldn't read him. Something had shifted between them at the hospital. It was getting more and more difficult for Star to remember the boy he'd been and easier for her to like the man he was now, yet a part of her didn't trust him or his motives.

Ron leaned over to pour more merlot into Star's glass.

"This is nice," he said. "A little downtime is what we all need."

"So true," Trudy agreed with a smile. She sipped her herbal tea.

The warmth of the day still hung in the air, settling around them like a soft whisper. Large red geraniums hung from planters attached to the eave of the back porch. Monster flowers. They just didn't grow like that anywhere but Alaska, home of the midnight sun.

Star leaned back in her chair, feeling sated and happy. "Dinner was wonderful. It's been ages since I've had beef stew and cornbread."

"Thanks," Trudy said. "It was easy. I made it ahead in the crockpot."

Star took another sip of her wine. "I know I should get home and get back to work on Patsy's place, but it feels so good to sit and do nothing."

"It's been a stressful couple of days," Trudy reminded her. "You're allowed."

Star stole another glance at Cade. His eyes held a predatory glow. Was he really that handsome, or was the wine she'd consumed making him look better than he really did? Unsettled, she focused on Trudy.

The back door opened, and Brad poked his head out. "Hey. I got Star's show on TV. Come look."

"I love that show." Trudy pushed to her feet.

They all filed into the house, even the twins, but instead of following them into the family room, Cade detoured, taking the kids upstairs to get ready for bed. Star couldn't help but feel a little relieved that Cade wasn't going with them to watch the show. Her stomach tightened a little at the thought of Cade critiquing her work. *Update This!* was her baby and she was more than a little invested in the show.

In the family room, Trudy, Ron, Star, and Brad crowded onto the two leather sofas. Brad picked up the remote control and turned up the volume.

Vivienne's French accent sang from the screen. "The color

will make the walls pop," she said as she removed the lid from a can of paint. "See?" She revealed a beautiful shade of what Star liked to call Sea Blue. "Blue and white looks so fresh and clean. So modern."

Vivienne dipped a paintbrush into the can and stroked the color onto the wall.

"I love that color," Trudy said in a dreamy voice.

Star pointed to the TV. "Vivienne can take the most rundown home and turn it into something spectacular. She did the design for Evan's place."

"I'd love for her to get her hands on this house," Trudy said. "The plumbing leaks. The windows are drafty. The kitchen is hopelessly outdated. Need I continue?"

Ron laughed. "You're right. But the place is ours, babe."

"She's hot." Brad pointed at Vivienne.

"Who's hot?" Cade asked as he came into the room.

"The designer chick on Star's TV show." Brad gestured toward the TV.

Cade glanced at the television with interest. He sat down beside Star and she moved over to make room for him. His thigh pressed to hers, they watched the wrap-up of the newly remodeled home, a seventies ranch-style house.

"That house was gorgeous, Star," Trudy said when the show ended. "And you're right. The designer did stay true to the original vision of the house."

"What's your job exactly?" Cade asked. "You're not on camera, are you?"

"No," Star said. "I'm production. I put the segments together. Make the arrangements. I do all the legwork, book the hotel, the catering, I even scout thrift stores and look for unique places to shop. I also help choose which houses are featured."

"What do you look for?" Trudy asked.

"Good architecture. Good family stories."

"What a glamorous job," Trudy said wistfully.

"Are you hinting that your life's not glamorous?" Ron asked with a grin.

Trudy laughed. "I wouldn't say my life is glamorous, but I like it just fine." She reached for Ron's hand. "I have you. You're all I want."

Envy moved through Star. Until now, she'd never missed having a close relationship with a man, but being here, watching Brandi and Bud, and now, Ron and Trudy, she couldn't help but wonder what it would be like to have someone care about her that much, to have a partner to help her wade through life.

"You're based in Seattle, right?" Ron asked.

"That's right. I just bought a brand new condo in the city. My very own dream house."

Trudy sighed. "Lucky girl."

Yes, lucky girl. Beside her, Cade shifted, the pressure of his thigh to hers increasing. A tiny flutter of sexual awareness sparked inside her.

Disturbed by her attraction to Cade, she said, "It's getting late. I should get home." Star stood, eager to put some distance between herself and Cade.

"I'll walk you," Cade insisted. "It's not safe this late. There's a pair of bears in the area. I wouldn't want you to come upon them alone, especially without your gun." He winked at her.

She didn't want to come upon the bears either. "Okay." She was pretty sure being alone with him was a bad idea, especially with her wine enhanced feelings, but she ignored the warning voice in her head and said, "Can I help you with anything before I go, Trudy?"

"I'll help her," Ron said, rising. "You two go on."

"Good night then." She waved to Brad. "See you tomorrow?" Brad was coming over tomorrow afternoon to help her move boxes—part of his punishment for getting caught drinking and vandalizing the night before.

"Yep," he said, his attention back on the television, his fingers working the remote control.

"Okay then." Star left the room, Cade behind her.

"I really can make it home on my own," Star said to him.

"I did it last night. It's not like I've never seen a bear before."

"It wasn't as late last night." Cade opened the door for her. "You're an independent, career woman. I get that. But I can use the fresh air. Let me walk you, Star."

They left the house, crossed the driveway, and started down the path that would take them from Cade's to Patsy's.

Star walked ahead of Cade. Knowing he watched her made her skin tingle, made her feel alive in a way she didn't quite understand or want to acknowledge.

When they reached the mobile home, Star went up the steps. "Hey," she said, when she noticed the broken window had been boarded up. "Did you do that?"

"I sent Brad over," Cade said. "Part of his punishment."

"Thanks." The unexpected kindness warmed her. "Thanks for dinner. And thanks for walking me."

Cade reached around her and opened the door.

For once, Star wished for darkness. Was he going to kiss her? No, that would be too weird. Her cheeks heated. Instinctively, Star back-stepped.

Cade reached for her, his hands closing around her upper arms. "Cold?" He rubbed her arms.

Was he kidding? If anything, her skin was heating up. "No."

"Me, either," he said, the double meaning clear. "Do I scare you, Star?"

"Not exactly. Well, maybe a little."

A shadow crossed his features. "I want to apologize again for the way I treated you when we were kids. I can't tell you how much I regret hurting and embarrassing you."

His hands slid up and down her upper arms, his touch gentle, sensual. He looked her straight in the eyes and Star saw sincerity and regret.

"Let's not talk about the past anymore," she said, unable to think of anything else to say. In fact, she was having trouble thinking at all as Cade's hands moved to her shoulders. "Let's just agree that we both had it rough and move on."

"Deal." His hands cupped her face. Slowly, his fingers

passed over her cheeks and into her hair.

No one had ever touched her like this, with such tenderness. Desire shot through Star. She felt like a piece of chocolate left too long in the sun, melted and delicious. Unable to help herself, Star swayed toward him.

His mouth took hers.

And heaven help her, Star kissed him back. He held her head in his large hands, making her a willing captive. She didn't want to escape. She wanted more. His tongue touched hers. Liquid heat pooled deep in her belly. For the first time she understood lust and longing.

Star inched closer to him, her hands splaying against his chest, so solid and firm under her palms. So male. So different from her.

Cade's mouth left her lips to explore her neck. Star moaned. His lips brushed over her chin, back to her mouth, and he whispered, "I always wanted to kiss you. That was a long time coming."

His words feathered across her skin, dissolving the rest of her doubts about this new improved Cade. She pulled back in an effort to gather her wits. Her heart pounded in her chest. Every nerve ending in her body sizzled.

He touched his forehead to hers. "I want you, Star. Maybe I always have."

Was this about sex? Did he want to have sex with her? "No, that's not happening."

"Why?" he asked.

Cade was a dead-end, for so many reasons. "I'm leaving soon."

"So?" he said, his eyes smoldering with intent. "We're grownups."

"Meaning?" she asked.

"Meaning we're free agents. We can make love without guilt."

Star turned out of his embrace, cold where she'd been hot seconds before. "Maybe you can, but I can't. I'm not a one-night stand kind of girl. We're not a good fit, you and I.

You're the all-American outdoorsman. I'm a city girl. We are worlds apart."

"Come on, Star," Cade said, taking her hands. "I'm talking about sex, no strings. I know you don't fit in here. If you were going to be here longer, well, who knows, but you're not. I'm just being realistic."

"I think the kiss was a bad idea." With a heavy heart, Star pulled her hands free and stepped through the open doorway. "I'm not looking for a one-night stand." She smiled sadly.

Cade took a step toward her. "Star."

Star held both hands up. "I'm sorry. I can't." She closed the door. She waited, half expecting him to knock, a part of her hoping he would, but he didn't. When she finally got up the nerve to look out the window, he was gone, leaving her to come to the conclusion that it really wasn't her he wanted, it was sex.

And sex was something she just wasn't good at, something she didn't know how to give, something she didn't understand. Maybe he could be casual about sex, but she couldn't. She needed the promise of something more than a casual affair to give her virginity away. She hadn't held on to her virginity all these years to give it away on a one-night stand to a man she didn't want a future with.

For years she'd watched her mother sleep with man after man. Star didn't want that. No wonder she didn't believe in happy endings. Relationships didn't last. They burned out. Love faded. Marriages dissolved.

There was no way she was going to turn into her mother, five times divorced, brokenhearted, and always searching for a man to make her feel better.

No, she was better off alone.

Cade O'Brien was a dead end road for her and from now on, she planned to stay far, far away from him.

* * *

Evan Jenson was exactly what Star had expected: a devilishly handsome rogue, dressed in a beige and navy plaid shirt he'd probably ordered from REI, and jeans that hugged his butt in a way that said they were his favorite pair. He wore his blond hair long, the layered strands brushing the tops of his shoulders. The look worked for him. Why someone hadn't snapped him up before now, Star had no idea.

She took the cup of coffee he offered her, her second, and set it in front of her on the table. "Are you okay with everything we've talked about so far?"

He slid into the seat opposite her. "So far, so good, pretty lady."

He had gorgeous eyes, eyes the color of rich brown velvet. Star had to admit he was even better looking in person. And charming. She was certain he'd charmed the panties off of dozens of women, maybe hundreds. He was definitely the type of guy she stayed far away from.

Star took a sip of her coffee, trying to ignore all the testosterone in the room. This was business. She had to stay in control. "You're okay with us setting up the tent out front?"

"Fine." His stare bored into her.

"Any questions about the design?" she asked, glancing up from her notes.

He shook his head, as if breaking free from a trance. "Yeah. I do have a couple of questions."

"I can have Vivienne call you," Star suggested.

"She's the French girl, right?" Evan grinned. "Yeah, have her call me. I'd like that."

Holy cow, the man had sex on the brain.

"Okay." She jotted his request down in her notebook. "The crew will arrive two weeks from Monday. They'll be here for one week."

"Are you part of the crew?" He winked at her.

"Nope. I'll be back in the office then. I'm preproduction." Star shut her notebook, and then put her digital camera back in the case.

"That's too bad," he drawled. "You busy tonight?"

"I have a date with a sixteen-year-old. We're packing up

my aunt's place."

"He's kind of young for you, isn't he?" Evan said with a grin meant to disarm.

Her mouth twisted into a wry smile. "Not when it comes to manual labor. Brad will do just fine."

"Marissa's kid?" Evan said suddenly sober.

"Do you know him?"

"Only in passing, but I knew Marissa. She had a screw loose."

"What do you mean?" Star's fingers tightened on her pen.

Evan tapped his head. "She was cuckoo. Nuts. She drove her car into the lake on purpose, you know."

"What?" Star asked, struggling to wrap her mind around his words.

"She had the two little ones with her. Could have killed them. The older one was in school. Guess he was lucky."

Lucky? Star's stomach rolled. Poor Brad.

"Yeah," Evan said. "Marissa kept running away to the city, and Cade'd go and drag her back. She hated it here. But to try and take your kids with you when you're trying to off yourself?" He shook his head. "She was one messed up chick."

Star packed up her notebook, shoving it into the pocket of her computer case. She didn't want to hear any more. Just thinking about Finn and Emma in the car with their distraught mother tugged on her heartstrings. Dear Lord, what had Cade and those kids been through? No wonder Brad was such a mess.

"I think we're done." She stood.

Evan rose, hooking his thumbs in his belt loops. "Are you sure I can't change your mind about dinner?" The hungry way he looked at her made Star wonder if she'd be the main course.

"No, thank you." She started for the door. "Call me if you have any questions."

She practically ran Evan down in her haste to get out of his house. She got in her car but she didn't start the engine right away.

Cade's wife had killed herself. It was all so sad, so senseless. How had Cade survived such a tragedy? In an instant, she knew—the kids. He'd gone on for them.

Star started the car. Cade was getting under her skin, no doubt about it. She needed to keep her distance from him. Between them they had enough baggage to keep a psychiatrist in business for years. Not a good thing. Definitely not a good thing.

* * *

Later that afternoon, after a visit with Brandi and baby Will, Star watched Brad as he packed the last of the kitchen utensils into a box. The tiny kitchen had been stripped of everything Patsy. Gone was the tin sign that had hung over the stove that read *Cooking On Low Is For Sissies*, gone was the cookie jar shaped like a big apple, and the macramé owl that hung in the kitchen window. Patsy's trademark ashtrays were packed up. The Coke glasses, free at the local gas station with a fill-up during the sixties, were stored away, bound for the local thrift shop. The old, worn avocado green countertops looked even sadder minus the usual clutter.

They'd been hard at it for a couple of hours now, working like dogs.

"Where do you want this box, Star?" Brad asked.

"Put it by the front door." Star tossed the dishrag she held onto the kitchen counter. "Does it look like we're going to have enough boxes to pack up the rest of the clothes?"

Brad set the box down. "Yeah. What about all the stuff in the other room?"

"You mean the paintings?" Star picked up the roll of packing tape.

"Yeah." Brad tossed his head to get his hair out of his eyes. He needed a haircut, but she wasn't going to tell him. That was Cade's job.

"I want to go through them," she said.

"What if there's one I want?" Brad's eyes met hers. He was

ready to do battle, everything from the stubborn set of his jaw to the way he held his body said so.

"Is there one you want, Brad?"

He nodded.

"Okay, come on." Star passed him, going to the spare bedroom. The room was stuffed with easels and canvases, large and small. Patsy's paints and brushes were stacked helter-skelter on a cheap six foot folding table, pushed up against the far wall.

"Which one?" Star asked, not sure where even to start digging.

Brad cut a path through the chaos, walking directly to a group of paintings leaning against the wall, under the window. He flipped several canvases forward before removing one of the larger paintings.

Star went to him. "What did you choose?" She took the canvas from him. A woman's face stared back at her, a beautiful face with clear green eyes, a straight nose, and a mouth with full lips. Her hair was auburn, the same shade as Emma's.

"Your mother," Star said.

Brad nodded.

"She was beautiful."

Brad stared at the portrait, then reached out to touch his mother's face. "Yeah."

Star's heart went out to him. "Of course you may have it. I'm surprised Patsy didn't already give them to you. Are there others here?"

Brad nodded.

"Take them, please," Star said.

He nodded again.

Star reached out and gave his arm a comforting squeeze. He didn't acknowledge the gesture and she hadn't expected him to.

Curious about Patsy's other paintings, Star began to flip through them. There were several landscapes, depicting everything from downtown Seward, to Resurrection Bay, to

Patsy's own yard. Star set aside a particularly stirring painting of Resurrection Bay, the sky gray, the water even grayer. Snow lined the pier, softened the businesses nestled nearby. She'd managed to capture the bay in winter, right down to the lonely gulls. The landscapes were raw and powerful, but the portraits stirred something in Star's soul.

Star recognized all of Patsy's subjects. There were several of Star, Tawney, Ruby Sue, and Brandi. There was even a wedding portrait of Brandi and Bud, which Star would make certain her sister received. There was one of Emma alone, and one with Emma, Finn, and Brad.

"This is why you come here, you and Finn and Em," Star said. "You come to see the paintings, don't you?" Her heart ached for the kids.

Brad nodded.

"Does your dad know?"

"I guess." Brad shrugged. "I asked if we could have them, and he said that they belonged to Patsy's estate."

"Well as the executor of Patsy's will, I'm giving them to your family. Take them all."

Brad gave her a small smile. "Thanks, Star." Brad held up a painting.

It was a portrait of Cade's father, Dan O'Brien. He'd been a handsome man, big and rugged and blustery. He'd died about a year before Patsy. Cancer. She remembered that much from Patsy's phone calls. "That's your grandpa."

"I know."

"Take it, too," Star said, certain Cade would want it.

"Dad won't want it," Brad said.

"Why not?" she asked, looking at Brad.

"Because of Patsy." Brad set the painting down.

"What do you mean?" Star asked, not understanding. "I think Cade would love it. It's good."

Brad shook his head. "Grandpa and Patsy were, you know, doing it."

"Doing what?" She stared at Brad, hoping she misunderstood.

"*It.*"

Did he mean sex? No. No way. She thought back. No, she'd never seen Patsy with Cade's father, not in any kind of romantic way. Patsy had worked for Dan O'Brien. She hadn't slept over, and he'd never stayed over with Patsy. Not once.

"Are you saying your grandpa and Patsy were dating?" she asked.

"I guess. I used to hear Dad and Uncle Ron arguing about it. Dad wanted to kick Patsy off our land after Grandpa died, but Uncle Ron wouldn't let him. He said that Grandpa made it clear that Patsy could live here as long as she wanted. Dad called Patsy a tramp."

Star bristled. "A tramp? Patsy wasn't a tramp. She was the most generous, loving person I've ever met." She struggled to process everything Brad had told her. "If she was friends with your grandpa, that was a choice they both made. Maybe they loved each other."

Brad shrugged. "Whatever. But I don't think Dad will want the painting."

"I'll tell you what," Star said. "I'll talk to him."

She'd talk to him all right and not just about the painting. She wanted him to take back his slanderous remark about Patsy. Dating a man didn't make a woman a tramp. What kind of caveman-type thinking was that? Thank goodness she'd made it clear their kiss was a one time lapse in judgment.

Brad tucked several canvases of his mother and siblings under his arms. "It's your funeral."

He left the room, leaving Star alone with a room filled with the people and places that had filled Patsy's life. Feeling a little haunted by her aunt, Star followed Brad out.

"Come on, Brad," she said. "I think you've done enough today. Put your paintings in the car and I'll give you a lift home."

CHAPTER SEVEN

The guests were gone.

Cade had a rare moment, a moment with no clients, no kids, no pressing work. He slung himself into the hammock positioned between the hemlock trees in the back yard, letting the canvas cradle his body. He released a contented sigh as the sun seeped into his bones. Around him, the air was still. The twins had gone into town with Trudy and Ron. Brad was over at Star's place.

He was alone.

Blissfully alone.

Cade closed his eyes. The buzz of a lone bee filled the silence and he concentrated on the hum. Man, this was living.

He tried to focus, to keep his mind blank, but Star seeped into the peace like he knew she would, like she had since returning to Alaska. Star, his guilty pleasure. Her mouth. Her legs. That body. Cade imagined every inch of her, first with clothes on, then with her clothes off.

In his imagination she was beautiful. The perfect woman.

He could still taste the sweetness of her mouth; feel her lush curves pressed against him. He wanted her. Bad. So badly his body coiled tight with need for her to the point of physical pain. Then he remembered her rejection, but even that didn't cool his raging hormones. He hadn't expected her

62

to trust him so quickly, to give in so easily. But a guy could wish. Never mind she didn't want kids. What did it matter? She wouldn't be sticking around anyway.

The whir of a car's engine broke through his thoughts. Cade groaned. He'd only been in the hammock for five minutes. He'd hoped for more alone time.

The engine cut. Two car doors opened then closed.

The front door of the house smacked shut.

And still he didn't move. How long before they discovered him?

"Cade?" Star called.

His eyes jerked open.

She was here—his fantasy.

"I'm sorry, did I wake you?" she asked.

Was it his imagination or was her tone a little frosty? He could see her now. A white T-shirt clung to her breasts. Her long legs were poured into form fitting jeans. She wore the yellow flip flops again, and he remembered how pretty her toes looked, topped with pink nail polish.

His body went on red alert.

"Can I talk to you?" she asked.

"Sure." Cade sat up, when he really wanted to invite her to climb into the hammock with him. Although, he was pretty sure she'd decline the invitation.

"I need to ask you something."

Cade rolled out of the hammock and onto his feet. "Okay." The serious look on her face cooled his libido. "Is it Brad? Did he do something?"

"No. He's great. He's inside."

Cade motioned for Star to follow him to the two lawn chairs parked in the shade of the hemlocks. "Have a seat."

"Thanks."

"What's wrong?"

"Nothing," she said a bit too quickly. "When Brad and I were cleaning out Patsy's place we found a bunch of her paintings. There are several of your late wife and your children. Brad asked if he could have them and I said yes. I hope that's okay."

"I knew about the paintings," Cade said. "I came home early once, and caught her painting Marissa and the kids."

"Why didn't you just ask me for them?" Her forehead wrinkled.

"I don't need anything from Patsy Cooper." The words popped out of his mouth before he could call them back. He prayed Star wouldn't notice the malice that spewed out with them.

"That's a weird thing to say."

Cade glanced away from her, from the questions he could see in her eyes.

"What's going on?" she asked. "There's a painting of your dad. When I told Brad to take it, he said you wouldn't want it. Why?"

His feelings for Patsy were twisted and complicated, many of them leftovers from a childhood filled with sorrow and grief.

"Were they lovers?" Star asked. "Your dad and Patsy?"

"I guess you could say that." Cade sighed. "I don't want to fight with you, Star. It's all in the past now, remember? Why rehash it?"

"Brad said you called Patsy a tramp. Explain that to me, O'Brien."

He could hear the hurt in her voice, see the pain on her face. He was back to square one with her. Damn. "Brad needs to keep his mouth shut." Cade's hands curled into fists. "After my mom died, my dad became friendly with Patsy."

"That doesn't make her a tramp," Star said defensively. "They were adults. Adults have relationships."

Cade exhaled. "I had a hard time when my mom died. My dad took her death hard. He pulled away from us. I was twelve years old. I needed him and I didn't understand why he wasn't available to me. One day when he left the house, I followed him. I caught my dad with Patsy at her place. After that, the rest of my world fell apart. My dad spent all his time with her; at least it seemed that way to me. I needed him. Ron needed him. He only needed Patsy."

"I never saw your dad with Patsy," Star said.

"He didn't go over there when Patsy had you and your sisters, but believe me they still snuck around."

Star shook her head. "You hated Patsy, didn't you? You hated her for stealing a piece of your dad."

"Pretty much." He was in so deep now, it didn't matter if he told her everything. "I didn't understand. I thought she was taking my dad away from me. And later, when I learned he was letting her live on our land, in our mobile home, rent free in exchange for her services—well, let's just say I had a hard time getting past that."

"Her services?" Star said, the words bitter, angry. She stood. "She worked for your family after your mother died. Come to this century, O'Brien. So what if she was living there rent free? So what if they didn't get married? We can't begin to guess the dynamics of their relationship. Maybe *you* are the reason they didn't marry. No one knows better than me how angry you were." Star's eyes widened. "I get it now. The harassment, it wasn't about me at all. You couldn't strike out at your dad or Patsy, so you took your anger out on me. Everything's so clear now."

Cade stood so he could look into Star's eyes. Shame washed over him. "Every time I looked at you, or your mother or sisters, I got angry. Your sisters were too young for me to bother with, but not you. You were a walking, talking reminder of the woman my dad was sleeping with. The more I picked on you, the more you looked at me like I was nothing, like you were better than I was. I had so much anger and no way to channel it. I wanted you to leave. All of you. Especially Patsy. I know I was wrong. I don't even have any defense. I was a screwed up kid, but Star, I'm not that kid anymore. You have to know how sorry I am."

"You keep saying that, yet, you're still angry with Patsy—a dead woman," Star said sadly. "I can hear the anger in your words, see it on your face. You haven't let the anger go. It's still inside you and no apology to me is going to make it go away."

"Star—"

"Stop talking. I don't want to hear any more." Star pivoted and walked away, her back ramrod stiff. She didn't say goodbye, not even to Brad who watched them from the back door.

"Way to go, Dad," Brad said after Star disappeared around the corner of the house. Brad went back inside, letting the door bang shut behind him.

Cade sucked in air. He wished he could just let Star go, but he couldn't. He'd brought her here. Now he'd hurt her again by venting his feelings. When would he ever learn? How would he make her understand that the past didn't matter? He understood his dad's feelings for Patsy. He had the same feelings for Star.

For the first time, he understood wanting someone so much.

He wanted to smooth things over with Star. For years his behavior toward Star had burned a hole in his gut. And he knew why.

He'd fallen for her then, and he'd hated himself for wanting her in the exact same way his dad had wanted Patsy.

* * *

After her conversation with Cade, Star drove to town, needing a distraction. She drove straight to the Internet café and powered up her laptop, finding an email from Frank telling Star to check the local thrift stores for an old two-man saw Vivienne wanted for an art project.

She was on her way to the local thrift store when her phone rang.

"Hi, Mom."

"Hi, Star," Destiny said.

Star shifted the phone to her other ear. "What's up?"

"I've decided to come for a visit if your offer to pick up the plane ticket still stands."

"Really?" Surprise shot through Star, followed by a hefty

dose of Why? "What made you change your mind?"

"Can't a grandma want to see her grandbaby?" Destiny asked in a put-out tone.

"Sure, Mom, but you're hardly grandma material."

"Don't I know it," Destiny said in a sarcastic tone. "How soon can you book the flight?"

Was it her imagination or did her mother seem in an awfully big hurry to get out of Vegas?

"I'll make the reservation right away," Star said. "It would be great if you could be here when Brandi gets home tomorrow."

"All right then," her mother said. "I can't wait to kiss that baby."

"Okay. I'll call you back with the details."

The line went dead. Was Destiny sincere? Or did she have another reason for wanting to come to Alaska? Maybe Destiny would act like a mother for a change. With Destiny here, Star could conclude her business at Patsy's place, leave Brandi to their mother's care, and get the heck out of Alaska, putting some much needed distance between Cade and her. If she had her way, she'd never see him again. Things happened for a reason. She could leave here clean. No messy relationship with Cade to worry about.

She was better off alone. She liked her life just the way it was. She wouldn't change a thing.

CHAPTER EIGHT

Destiny Cooper White Johnson O'Hara Lamont Jones blew into town like a gale force wind—the kind that toppled trees and knocked out the power.

Star was waiting in baggage claim when she spotted her mom. Destiny's bleached blonde hair, too tight top stretched over her surgically enhanced breasts, courtesy of husband number four, Harry Lamont, and her painted on jeans made her hard to miss. As Destiny made her way through the crowd to the luggage carousel, male heads turned, some even snapped around so fast Star was sure the men got whiplash. And Destiny noticed. She thrived on the attention, turning her megawatt smile on any man stupid enough to think he might have a chance with her.

Star wanted to yell, "Run while you have the chance," to the men, but instead she called, "Hi, Mom."

"Starlene, there you are," Destiny said when she spotted Star. Star met her halfway, taking her mother's hot pink carry-on bag from her before giving her a one-armed hug.

"You look tired," her mother said with a frown. "You should give yourself a lift. Put some highlights in your hair. Smile more."

Star rolled her eyes. "I look tired because I am tired. I've been working and making the drive here to visit Brandi every day."

"You've always been a saint," her mother said with a tight smile. "So responsible. A real little mother when you were a girl. I never understood it. You certainly didn't get that from me."

"No kidding."

"Hey, Star."

Star turned at the sound of Cade's voice. Great. She had no desire to talk to him now, with her mother an avid onlooker. "O'Brien." She frowned. She hadn't seen him since their fight, and she didn't want to see him now.

"Star, aren't you going to introduce me?" Destiny asked, a predatory glow in her eyes.

"Oh, sorry. Mom, you remember Cade O'Brien."

"Cade O'Brien?" her mother said, the words gushing with pleasure. "Dan's son? Well, didn't you grow up to be a handsome man, just like your daddy." Her mother smiled, extending her hand, complete with hot pink acrylic nails, to Cade.

Star's stomach tightened. She didn't want her mother touching Cade, not even in greeting. And then it hit her. She was jealous, jealous of her own mother.

"Destiny." Cade took her mother's hand. "Nice to see you again."

Destiny practically purred. Star wanted to puke. Cade pulled his hand free.

"What're you doing here?" Star asked Cade.

"Picking up clients." He focused his attention on Star now. "Their flight arrives in about five minutes. We could have carpooled. I don't have to ask why you're here."

"Mom came to see Will," Star offered, although she wasn't sure why she was telling him anything.

"It's true, I did," Destiny said. "I couldn't stay away."

"Of course not," Cade replied his tone congenial. He looked to Star. "We're having a fish fry tomorrow night. Why don't you and your mother come for dinner?"

Before Star could say, fat chance, her mother said, "We'd

love to. Wouldn't we, Star?"

"I don't know," Star hedged, rummaging for a plausible excuse. She couldn't watch her mother paw Cade all evening. She'd rather chew broken glass. "Brandi—"

Her mother cut her off. "Will be fine without us for the evening. Unlike you, she does have a husband, remember?"

Destiny gave Cade her killer smile. "What time should we be there, Cade?"

Star's stomach rolled. Her mother was hitting on Cade. Good grief.

Cade grinned. "Six o'clock."

"We'll be there." Destiny gave him another man-eating smile.

Thankfully the luggage began spouting out and landing on the conveyor belt with a thud.

"Come on, Mom." Star took her mother's arm. "The bags are coming."

"We'll see you later, Cade," Destiny said with a wink.

"I'm looking forward to it," Cade said, his eyes on Star.

Star led her mother to the luggage carousel.

"What's your suitcase look like?" Star asked.

"It matches my carry-on. It's hot pink."

As if on cue, a hot pink suitcase popped out through the opening. Star hefted the bag from the carousel. "Come on, Mom, let's go."

"You're always in a hurry, Star. Chill out."

Star walked from baggage claim. She didn't even look to see if her mother followed or not. They'd only been together for minutes and Star was annoyed already.

Once they were in the car and on the road, Star said, "Brandi's really excited to see you, Mom."

"I can't wait to see her." Destiny looked out the window. "I swear I've never understood the appeal here. All this green. All the rain. All the snow."

"Come on, Mom," Star said. "Admit it's beautiful country. Seward is gorgeous. Where else can you get a three hundred and sixty degree view of the mountains? And the bay. I mean,

I'm not Alaska's number one fan, but even I can't deny the beauty."

"If I remember correctly, the town reeks of fish," her mother said, her nose wrinkling.

"True," Star agreed. "I guess it's a tradeoff."

"I'll take the desert any time." Destiny gave her a tight smile. "So how long are you staying on?"

"I'm pretty much done with Patsy's place," Star told her. "I'm supposed to be back in Seattle a week from Monday. I've been working from here, but I'm nearly finished. Brandi wants me to stick around, but I'd like to leave sooner."

"You're such a Cosmo girl." Her mother smiled. "I envy you, Star."

"Really?" Star asked, surprised.

"Of course. You've always known what you wanted. You're a go-getter."

"I guess."

"What's Cade's story?"

Star bristled. "Don't you think he's a little young for you?"

Her mother laughed while at the same time managing to toss her long, blonde hair. "I wasn't asking for myself. I'm thinking of you, Star. Is he married?"

"No, but if you're thinking of trying to make a match between me and Cade, forget it. That will never happen. We have too much history, all of it bad. Plus, he's got three kids."

"Oh." Destiny frowned. "Three kids? That makes him a little less appealing. But he's handsome, you have to admit it. I've never understood why you didn't get along with him."

Star glanced at her mother. "He was mean to me. He hated Patsy. He told me that recently. And he told me other things."

"What things?" her mother asked, turning to look at Star, her overly waxed eyebrows raised.

"He told me that his father let Patsy live in the mobile home rent free. He basically implied she got free rent in exchange for sex."

"They had an arrangement. So what?" Destiny asked with

a hair flip. "Star, don't look so shocked. It was hardly a secret. Dan and Patsy were adults. He was her boss and her lover."

"I never knew."

"Honey, does it really matter?" her mother asked in a soft voice. "Patsy was a saint with a heart of gold. So what if Dan O'Brien paid her rent? Maybe it was a job perk. That sounds so archaic. Dan had money to burn and he wanted to take care of her. He loved her. He knew it would be upsetting to the boys if he married her. Patsy was good with the arrangement. They were exclusive. It was a win-win for everyone."

"I get that. I just feel stupid for not figuring it out," Star said. "And you're right. Cade never would have accepted Patsy in the role of his stepmother. He hated her."

Destiny examined her glossy fingernails. "Then he's a fool. I couldn't have raised you girls without her help. Patsy kept food on the table for you kids when I couldn't. I'll never feel anything but gratitude and love toward her, and you should, too."

"I do love her, Mom," Star said. "It's Cade's twisted view of Patsy that bothers me."

"Surely Cade's grown out of that nasty little boy stage by now? He seemed perfectly nice at the airport. We all need a man, Star. Someone to take care of us. Someone to love. Put him on your radar, honey."

"Are you joking?" Star asked. "I just told you he spent most of his life hating me."

"You don't want to end up alone, Star," Destiny said, the words thick with desperation.

"Why not?"

"Because it's terrifying," Destiny said, as if Star were an idiot.

"Not for me."

"That's because you're young. Wait until you're older and facing the end of your life alone."

"That's your opinion, Mom. I'm stronger than that. If you and Patsy have taught me anything, you've taught me that I want to take care of myself. I'm never going to be kept by any man."

Destiny shook her head. "You're pretty self-righteous for a girl who's never been in love. Love is the ultimate drug, the best high in the world. That's why I've had five husbands. I didn't marry them so they could take care of me. I married them for love."

"I don't see it that way," Star said. "I've watched you go through so much heartache, Mom."

"And so much bliss." Destiny gave a short laugh. "I'll admit it. I'm addicted to love."

Star would never see eye to eye with her mother when it came to men.

They passed the rest of the drive with small talk. At the hospital, Star watched the reunion between Brandi and her mom, then Star gave baby Will a kiss and made her exit.

Being trapped in the car with Destiny had just about done her in. Star needed a break; even better, she knew just how she wanted to spend it.

* * *

Star's fingers tightened around the binoculars.

She fixed her sight on the eagle. In awe, she moved to the left, another eagle coming into view. So far she'd counted fifteen. How many times had she stood in this exact spot when she'd been a teenager? Eagle Ridge had been her place, her own private therapy session when she'd needed to remove herself from all things Destiny. Some things never changed.

She glanced at her watch. Almost four o'clock. She'd been at this for three hours. With regret, Star turned away, heading for her car.

After being with the eagles, she felt calmer, ready to face her mother, and she felt pretty sure she'd find Destiny waiting for her at the trailer. Brandi had offered to loan Destiny her car, leaving their mother free to come and go as she pleased.

When Star pulled into the driveway, she found Destiny

sitting on the front porch, smoking.

"Star," Destiny called with a wave of her cigarette. "Finally. Where on earth have you been?"

"Sightseeing." Star walked up the porch steps and let herself into the house. When her mom moved to follow, she said, "Leave the cigarette outside, okay?"

"Sure, sure, whatever." Destiny dropped the cigarette and ground it out under the heel of her cheap black boot. "This place is as dismal as I remember it."

Star set her purse on the counter.

"I never understood how Patsy could live here."

"Come on, Mom," Star said with a smirk. "The place was rent-free, remember?"

"Still." Destiny shook her head and stuck out her tongue.

A knock at the door brought both women around.

"Hey, Finn," Star said, surprised to see the little boy.

Finn squinted at Destiny. "Who're you?"

"Finn, this is my mom, Destiny."

"Hi, Finn," Destiny said with a smile. "Aren't you cute?"

"Finn is Cade's son," Star told her.

Destiny perked up. "Really? No wonder you're so handsome."

Finn looked down at his untied tennis shoes.

"What's happening?" Star asked, her tone light.

Finn's lower lip trembled. "Something's wrong with Trudy."

"What do you mean?" Star asked.

"She's sick or something."

"Is Ron with her?" Star asked, alarmed now.

Finn nodded. "At the hospital."

"What?" Star reached for her purse. "Come on, Finn. Get in the car. I'll take you home and find out what's going on."

"Who's Trudy?" her mother asked.

"Ron's wife."

"Oh, the other brother," Destiny said. "You're not leaving without me. I'll die of boredom if I have to stay here alone."

"Fine," Star said. "Everyone get in the car."

When they arrived at the O'Briens, the three of them made a beeline for the house. Emma sat on the front porch, Snowbell in her lap.

"Hey, Emma," Star said gently. "Is your dad inside?"

Emma nodded. "He's with the guests."

"Okay." Star pulled the screen door open. "Mom, stay here with Finn and Emma."

"But—" Destiny started to protest.

"Please, Mom," she snapped.

"Oh, all right." Destiny glanced at the kids, looking at them as if they were from outer space.

Star went inside. "Cade?"

"He's in the kitchen," Brad said, as he came down the stairs.

"What's going on with Trudy?" Star asked.

"I'm not sure. She wasn't feeling good or something. Uncle Ron took her to the doctor."

Star didn't like the sound of that. She'd just been through the ringer with Brandi. She hoped Trudy was okay.

"Star." The rich baritone of Cade's voice pulled her around. He strode to her, his brow creased.

"Finn came to my place. He told me something was wrong with Trudy."

"She was having contractions, but I just talked to Ron and they've got them stopped."

"So she's all right?" Star asked, her heart beating again.

"For now," Cade said, but his mouth moved into a grim line.

"That's a relief. Where does that leave you? Don't you have a house full of guests?"

He nodded. "It's barbeque for dinner tonight. Thank goodness Trudy had already made the salad and the dessert before the contractions started."

"Trudy's working too hard," Star said. "She needs to rest."

"Don't you think I know that?"

"Maybe you need to hire someone," she suggested.

"I've thought of that, too."

Star softened. "Look, I'm still mad at you, but I want to help Trudy. Can I fill in? I'm here. So's my mom. We could help get you through the evening."

A shadow crossed his features: hope, relief, or was he simply grateful for the offer?

"Why would you do that for me, Star?"

"Because it's the right thing to do. The neighborly thing."

He gave her a slow nod. "Okay. I could use the help, if it's not too much trouble."

"It's no trouble."

"Star, I'm sorry about the other day. You're right. I need to let go of the past."

"You do," she said. "Maybe we both do."

He touched her arm. "Star."

"Do you want my help or not?"

For a moment neither of them moved. He looked at her hard, as if he were trying to see inside her; then things changed. His stare grew hungry and a palpable need rose between them. Her neck felt too warm. Her stomach did a rollercoaster drop. What was happening to her? One more minute of this and she'd turn into a puddle on the floor.

Raucous laughter from the kitchen broke the spell.

Cade let go of her arm. "I better get back in there."

Star wanted to say she was right behind him, but her throat had closed up tight. Cade confused her. Just when she was prepared to dislike him, he said or did something to make her want him.

The rest of the evening went off without a hitch. To Star's surprise, Destiny was the perfect hostesses, setting the table, keeping the food moving, helping Cade keep the conversation flowing.

Destiny ate up the male attention, and the male guests, two middle aged men from Canada, couldn't get enough of Destiny. Destiny knew how to make a man feel special to the point it was painful for Star to watch her mother in action. So Star excused herself to do the dishes.

Cade also made his escape, taking the twins up to bed.

Star finished drying the last plate and put it in the cupboard with the others. Outside, she could hear her mother's tinkling laugher, the feminine sound blending with the male voices.

Cade walked into the kitchen. He surveyed the room. "You're fast. I was going to offer to help, but I see I'm too late."

Star smiled. "Yep, I'm done." She folded the dishtowel and set it on the counter.

"You've gone above and beyond the call of duty," Cade said. "I really appreciate everything you and your mom did for me tonight."

"No problem," Star said.

"You're a good person, Star."

"Don't read too much into my offer of help," Star said.

He gave her a tight smile. "I can always count on you to tell it like it is. I better get back out there before your mother eats our guests for dessert." He headed toward the door. "I do appreciate the help, Star. Besides, you're nice to have around. Real nice." And then he was gone.

Star didn't move. Her heart thudded in her chest. The blood in her veins had gone hot, making her warm all over. Why on earth would she be attracted to Cade? The man made her crazy. Yet, she couldn't deny the physical side of their relationship and that left her feeling out of control. Hopelessly out of control.

CHAPTER NINE

The following afternoon, Star found herself at the marina, watching for Cade's boat. She had agreed to pick the guests up and drive them back to the house. Although Trudy was back home, she was on bed rest, and Star had felt compelled to offer her help.

Star glanced at her watch. Almost three. She'd done her best to focus on her work all morning. She'd even managed to finish up the last minute tasks Frank had asked for and have another meeting with Evan.

Frank had also sent her the rough cut of the updated promo piece, and she'd viewed it, calling him with her approval. After that, she'd spent an hour on the phone with Vivienne listening to the designer's ideas, asking her about the requested saw. Vivienne intended to paint a picture on the saw of Evan's plane bobbing next to the dock, then hang the saw above the headboard on Evan's bed. Star thought the idea was clever, but she didn't think she could sleep with a saw hanging above her head. What if it fell? Yikes.

Star took a seat on the bench. From here, she had full view of the marina. The bay glistened in the sun. A gentle breeze blew just enough to keep the day from getting too hot.

Boats, some commercial fishing boats, others pleasure crafts, both sail boats and speed boats, bobbed gently in their slips. The air held the tang of salt and fish. The scent brought back memories of playing on the docks and eating fresh caught halibut and chips.

Two boats were headed in, one navy, the other white. She had no idea what Cade's boat looked like. The navy boat docked, but the driver was an older guy. The second boat came in behind it, and as the boat approached, she recognized Cade through the cabin window.

He docked the boat like an expert, then exited the cabin. His voice reached her ears as he gave Brad orders. Star enjoyed the view. Few men could fill their clothes the way Cade did. Even windblown he was rugged and sexy.

The clients left the boat. Star rose to meet them.

"Hello, Star," the man named Ernie called when the group spotted her. If she remembered correctly, Ernie was in real estate, and his friend, John, was a medical doctor. Both men were in their early fifties, graying, but still fit and nice looking.

She waved. "How was fishing?"

"Excellent." John gave her a salute. "We all limited."

"That's wonderful." Star smiled. "The van is parked right there. I'm going to drive you gentleman back to the B & B."

"Good enough," Ernie said.

Star waited as the men filed by.

Cade jogged up the gangplank to her. "Hey. Is everything okay? Why are you here?"

His obvious concern softened her. "Relax. I went by to see Trudy and offered to help. She sent me here."

"Ah. I see." He seemed to drink her in. "Looks like I owe you another one."

"Looks like it," she shot back, unable to squash the excitement Cade made her feel. "You better hope I don't collect."

Cade grinned. "I'll take my chances."

Her stomach lurched. Were they flirting? Why couldn't she remain neutral around him? Why did her pulse have to roar? "I need to go. The guys are waiting."

Still smiling, he said, "I'll see you tonight."

JOLEEN JAMES

Star looked at him blankly.

"The fish fry," he reminded her. "You said you'd come, remember?"

"Destiny said we'd come, not me."

"Come on, Star," Cade coaxed. "Don't make me beg." His eyes crinkled at the corners with mischief.

Star broke a smile. "Would you beg? Because that's a sight I'd pay to see."

"You know I would." Warmth infused the words. Suddenly it was too intimate between them.

"I need to go," Star said, backing away from him.

His smile doubled. He knew he flustered her!

"See you tonight, Star."

With a shake of her head, Star walked away, all too aware of Cade's stare on her back.

* * *

"Star, you're a lifesaver," Trudy said.

Star glanced up from the salad she'd just set on the table in time to see Ron walk by with Trudy in his arms. He placed his wife in a padded lounge chair, carefully, as if she were made of fine crystal.

Star watched the exchange between Trudy and Ron with envy. They loved each other so much.

"I mean it, Star," Trudy said as she made herself comfortable. "We couldn't have managed without you yesterday or today."

"Trudy's right," Ron said. "We owe you big." He kissed his wife's forehead before heading over to the concrete patio where Cade messed with the large, outdoor deep fryer.

"No thanks necessary." Star smiled.

Trudy grinned back, her fingers laced protectively over her large belly.

"Are you feeling okay?" Star sat in the chair beside Trudy's. "Can I get you anything?"

"Nope, I'm fine. Just glad to be home."

Destiny exited the house, a steaming pot of corn on the

cob in her hands. John and Ernie trailed after her like lovesick school boys. Yuck. Star frowned.

"Your mother sure is good for business," Trudy said with wonder. "The men love her."

Star frowned. "They do."

"Has she been spending much time with your sister?"

"Some, but babies really aren't Mom's thing."

Trudy chuckled. "No, I guess not."

"Who wants wine?" Destiny held up a bottle.

"Me," Ernie said, followed by an "I do" from John.

"Star?" her mother said, wiggling the bottle in time with her hips.

"No, thanks. I'll take an ice tea though." No wine enhanced feelings for her tonight. She wanted to deal with Cade with a clear head.

Destiny began filling the glasses. Ron returned with a glass of water for Trudy.

Brad came around the corner of the house, Finn and Emma following behind. As usual, Emma had Snowbell in her arms.

When Emma saw Star, she broke away from the boys.

"Star. Look what I got." She ran to Star. Snowbell landed in Star's lap with a meow. "Daddy bought me a pretty collar for her."

A pink collar with a tiny silver bell circled Snowbell's neck.

"It's beautiful." Star fingered the bell. "I love it."

Emma nodded enthusiastically. "I love it, too."

"It's girly," Finn grumbled. He reached for the salad and plucked a cherry tomato from the bowl.

"Finn," Trudy exclaimed with horror. "We don't know where those hands have been. Go inside and wash up. You, too, Emma."

"Okay." Emma ran for the house, followed by Finn who moved at a much slower pace.

Star was left holding Snowbell. The kitten curled up into a ball. Star ran her hand over the fur. "She's so soft."

"She's a sweet cat," Trudy agreed.

"I see you have a new friend," Cade said as he joined them. He smiled at Star, and again, his handsomeness made her insides sizzle.

She stroked the kitten to cover her wild reaction to him. "I guess I do."

"Here, Star." Destiny passed her a glass of ice tea. She looked pointedly at Cade. "What can I get you, handsome?"

"How about a beer?" Cade said without blinking at the endearment. "There's a cooler full near the door."

Destiny smiled. "Back in a jiff." She sashayed away, her painted on jeans leaving nothing to the imagination.

Both Ernie and John paused to watch Destiny in action. Star stifled a grown. She wondered if the men were married. If not, she felt doubly sorry for them.

"I was just telling Star that her mother's a hit," Trudy said. "She'd be a perfect fill-in for me while I'm out of commission. Men love her. I know she's just here on vacation, but maybe she'd like to make a little extra money. What do you think, Cade?"

Before Cade could reply, Destiny returned with his beer. She passed it to him. "Here you go."

"Thanks." Cade took a long drink.

"What can I do next?" Destiny asked, totally oblivious to the unanswered question that hung in the air.

"Relax," Trudy said. "Go drink your wine. You were invited here for dinner, not to work." She smiled at Cade.

Cade gave Destiny a long perusal. Was he considering asking Destiny to work for him? If so, he was nuts. Her mother would tie the male guests in knots. There wasn't a man born yet who could resist the sex appeal that oozed from her.

Destiny patted Trudy's shoulder. "You're such a sweet girl. I think I'll go and chat with Ernie and John. Want to join me, Star?"

"I'm going to stay with Trudy." Star wasn't going anywhere until she heard Cade's response.

"Okay. Toodles." Destiny gave them a wave before

rejoining the men.

Cade took another sip of beer.

"Well, Cade?" Trudy asked. "She'd be perfect, don't you agree?"

As if on cue, John and Ernie burst out laughing at something her mother had said.

"Maybe," Cade said in a noncommittal way.

"What do you think, Star?" Trudy asked, her eyes bright with hope.

"I think you're insane. Mom's a man-magnet. I don't think you want the kind of trouble she has the potential to stir up."

Cade continued to observe her mother, a thoughtful expression on his face.

"What about you?" Trudy asked. "Would you consider filling in while you're here?"

Star shook her head. "I have a job."

"I'd like to ask your mother." Cade swiveled back to face Star. "Trudy's right. She's a natural."

Star's mouth dropped open. Never in a million years did she think Cade would go for Trudy's suggestion. He didn't like her mother, did he? Or was he as infatuated with her fake breasts as every other guy?

Trudy clapped her hands. "Great. Let's ask her after dinner."

Star took a big gulp of her ice tea, suddenly wishing she'd asked for wine. Her mother? Working for the O'Briens? Had everyone gone wacko?

"Ladies," Cade said. "I'm going to leave you to your drinks. The deep fryer is calling me."

"What's going on between the two of you?" Trudy asked when Cade was out of earshot. "Cade's looking at you like you're a chocolate chip cookie he wants to eat."

Star's cheeks heated. "He is not."

"Yes, he is. I haven't seen him look at anyone that way for a very long time." Trudy raised her eyebrows. "Are you interested?"

"No," Star said. "We have nothing in common. Besides,

I'm leaving soon."

"So?" Trudy laughed. "I can't believe I'm saying this, but have a fling. You don't need to marry Cade or raise his kids. Cade's a good guy. It's summer. There's magic in the air."

"Magic?" Star gave a dry laugh. "I think you're reading too many romance novels, Trudy."

"Whatever." Trudy shrugged. "I know sexual tension when I see it, and you and Cade have enough between you to set this place on fire."

Ron came toward them, a plate of fried fish in his hands. "Come eat, Star," he called, halting their conversation. Then, "I'll bring you a plate in a second, Trudy."

"Thank you, sweetie," Trudy said with a smile. "Go eat, Star. I'm good right here."

By the time Star got to the table, the only open seat was between Cade and Brad. Star stepped over the bench to squeeze in between the two O'Briens. Trudy's words still rang in her ears. Summer fling. Magic. Cade's thigh brushed hers. Her body came alive in response. Wanting to put some space between them, she inched closer to Brad but then bumped against his thigh. Not good. In the end, she leaned a little more in Cade's direction.

Big mistake. His hard, muscled thigh pressed along the length of hers. Heat infused her leg.

He leaned in and whispered, "You can sit as close to me as you want. I won't bite."

His breath tickled her neck, sent a tingle to her toes. Was he trying to seduce her? Did she want him to?

Somehow, Star made it through dinner with Cade's leg pressed to hers. Never in her life had she experienced this level of sexual awareness of another person. Desire tied her stomach in knots. No matter their past, she couldn't deny her attraction to him. She wanted him but at what cost to her pride? She wasn't tramp material and she never would be. How did one have a fling without feeling cheap?

Cade unfolded himself from the bench, holding his hand out to her. "Come on. I could use some help getting the coffee."

"All right."

Star glanced around. No one at the table was paying any attention to them. She took Cade's hand, and let him lead her from the table.

* * *

Cade loved the feel of Star's hand in his. Her smooth skin only added to his need for her, made him wonder what she'd feel like all over.

She looked up at him, her green eyes bright with arousal, an arousal he'd put there. She could deny her attraction to him all she wanted, but he knew better. He could read her easily. She wore her emotions on her face. Despite their past, she wanted him.

And he wanted her. On any terms. Truth be told, a fling suited him just fine. Star didn't want kids, and she sure didn't belong in Seward. She was a city girl, like Marissa had been. He'd already tried to keep a city girl here, with disastrous results. He had no intention of going down that road again.

He walked Star to the house, up the steps, inside.

Reluctantly, he let go of her to add water to the carafe and switch the pot on. Star stood near the sink, watching him.

"What're we doing, O'Brien?" Her tongue came out to wet her lips.

He advanced on her. "What do you want to do, Star? Whatever you want, I'm all for it."

Her eyes darkened and did a slow rove down his body. "I don't want anything," she said, the words hollow and false.

"Liar." Cade's body snapped to attention. "Something's happening between us and you can't deny it. I can't deny it. I don't want to deny it. You're the most beautiful, exciting woman I've ever known. Even when you hate me, I want you."

"I still hate you," she said, but the words didn't match the fire in her eyes.

"Baby, if that's hate I'm feeling, bring it on." He closed the gap between them.

She backed up, her butt hitting the edge of the counter.

Cade leaned in. This close, he caught her scent. Desire crashed through him.

"Back up." Her palms landed square on his chest. "You've got a yard full of people out there."

"I don't care." He needed to touch her, needed for her to feel the same way about him. Cade moved his hands to her waist, a tiny waist. She gasped softly. Slowly, he drew her to him. Her hands were still on his chest between them, yet they fit together like they were made for each other. Her eyes widened when he rocked against her and he knew she felt his arousal.

The coffee pot beeped three times.

"Coffee's ready," she said, but she didn't move away. Her lips parted, and he couldn't resist that lush mouth of hers.

Cade kissed her, mouth open, tongues mating. He gathered her to him. She tasted like summer, like sex, hot, naughty sex. His hands slipped under her shirt, and he stroked the satin skin of her back. Star's fingers curled into his shirt as if she were hanging on for dear life.

The coffee pot beeped again.

Cade broke the kiss, but he didn't back away.

She brought a hand to her lips. "Wow."

He grinned. "I hope that's good."

"You know it is, but I'm not so sure I should be kissing you."

He didn't want to lose the sexual buzz between them. "You think too much, Star. Let go. Have a good time. I won't tell anyone."

"Is that coffee ready?" Ron called as he clumped up the porch steps.

Star twisted out of his embrace.

"Yeah," Cade said, moving away to hide the bulge in his jeans from his brother.

"I'll get it," Star said, her voice unsteady. She was as ruffled as he was; he'd bet money on it.

Thankfully, Ron didn't come in, but did an about face and went back down the stairs.

Star pulled the pot of coffee out.

"We're not done yet." He faced her now. She held the coffee pot between them as if it were a weapon of protection.

"Meet me tonight."

She started for the door. "I can't. My mother—"

"Isn't keeping tabs on you," Cade said. "Have a summer romance with me, Star. No strings. I know; you're a modern girl. You don't want kids or attachments. That's okay with me. Whatever you want. Sleep with me. You won't be sorry."

Her brow wrinkled. "I told you, I'm not good at casual sex."

"Not true." He smiled. "You're very good."

Star pivoted away, taking the coffee outside.

Cade went to the kitchen sink and turned on the cold water, splashing some on his face. He needed a cold shower. Star set him on fire. Was he out of line asking her to have a summer fling with him? He hoped not, because deep down, he wanted more from her. How much more, he wasn't sure, but he knew that one week with her wouldn't be enough.

* * *

Star jerked awake, her eyes opening wide in the darkness. With a moan, she rolled over, but Patsy's couch was as hard as an old board. Star yanked the blanket up to her chin and tried to get comfortable.

It had taken her forever to fall asleep when they'd returned home after the fish fry; now she was wide awake. Why? The kiss? No, it was more of a full out seduction. Star touched her lips. Cade had opened a door for her tonight. She'd never thought of herself as a sexual being, but, boy-oh-boy, he'd shown her otherwise in his kitchen.

She'd wanted him, all of him. She still did. If he kept pouring on the charm, she'd give in. What did that say about her as a person? Where was her strict moral code? Obviously being wanton ran in her blood. Some people had doctors or lawyers in their families, she had sexy women, or more correctly, women who liked to have sex. She groaned.

Star flipped over, then she heard it, a male voice followed by her mother's soft laughter.

"You've got to be kidding," Star said.

Was her mother doing it with one of Cade's guests? Her mother really was a dedicated employee. She hadn't even had her first official day working for the O'Briens and she already had one of the men in bed. Star remembered her own kiss with Cade. Sexy women. Case closed.

This was worse than embarrassing. It was humiliating.

Star put her pillow over her ears. This wasn't the first time she'd had to listen while her mother entertained men, or serviced her current husband. Star's stomach turned at the memory of the scared little girl she'd been.

Star raised the pillow. She didn't hear anything now. After putting the pillow back under her head, she rolled onto her back, staring up at the smoke-stained ceiling.

Her mother really was a piece of work. No wonder Star was so screwed up and repressed when it came to sex. The bedroom door opened. Star closed her eyes.

Destiny giggled softly. "I'll see you tomorrow?"

"You couldn't keep me away."

John. The doctor. Star recognized his voice. Her mother was aiming high this time.

More rustling as Destiny walked him to the door. She opened the door quietly. Lips smacked as they kissed. The door clicked shut. Star sat up and turned on the light.

"Really, Mom."

Her mother whirled around, one hand on her chest. "Starlene. I thought you were asleep." Destiny's blonde hair was good and messed up. Clad in a short, black satin robe she looked every inch the aging sex kitten she was. "Sorry, sugar." Destiny tightened the belt around her waist. "I really like him." She plopped down on the couch at Star's feet. "He's nice. He has money."

"Slow down, Mom," Star said. "Did you even ask if he was

married?"

"Of course I did." She smiled the same stupid dreamy smile Star had seen on Destiny's face a million times. "He's divorced. His kids are grown."

"He lives in Canada, Mom."

"So what? I didn't tell you before, but now that Cade's offered me a job, I guess I'll come clean. I got fired. I'm tired of Vegas anyway. I'm ready for a change. Change is good, Star."

She couldn't believe she was going to have to talk her mother down. "Get real, Mom. What are you going to do? Stay here and work for Cade? Where are you going to live? He's tearing this place down. And I'm sure you don't want to stay with Brandi and Bud. Do you even have any money saved?"

Destiny pinned her with her "mother" stare. "You know, Star, it wouldn't hurt you to dream big. I mean, what do you really have in your life? A job and a slick condo won't keep you warm at night."

"So I'll buy an electric blanket. At least I can afford one."

Destiny jumped to her feet. "That was low, Star. You've never understood me. I'm going to bed." She whirled away.

"Keep it down this time," Star called after her. "Some of us are trying to sleep."

The bedroom door slammed.

A knot formed in Star's stomach. Her heart aching, she switched off the light.

CHAPTER TEN

Star woke up with a headache, the result of poor sleep. Her mother, who now worked for the O'Briens, had barely spoken to her before she'd left to help with breakfast, yet Star didn't regret the words they'd exchanged. Destiny needed to grow up. She was fifty-two. If anything, Star should be the one sneaking guys into her room. Catching your mother in the act was unnatural—something no child should have to witness, no matter how old the child was.

Star stood under the shower. Hot water soothed her pounding head. She was so done with Alaska, and she'd be glad when *Update This!* finished with this segment and she could put this God forsaken state out of her life, with hope, forever.

Star spent the morning working on production logistics for *Update This!* At noon, she grabbed a quick bite to eat before heading over to visit Brandi, who was home now. She spent the rest of the afternoon entertaining Will while Brandi took a nap. Star half expected Destiny to show up but wasn't surprised when her mother didn't come by. Why would she when she could use her job at Cade's as an excuse for staying away?

Still upset with her mom, Star didn't go home until she was sure Destiny would be at the O'Briens serving dinner.

When Star arrived at Patsy's she found the driveway empty. She let herself in to the quiet mobile home and kicked off her heels.

Hungry, she cruised through the meager contents of the fridge: milk, eggs, cheddar cheese, bottled water, a half a bottle of white wine, and a six pack of diet cola.

Star's stomach growled as she removed the eggs and cheese. An omelet was better than nothing.

The rattle of an engine pulled her around. Thinking it was too early for Destiny to be home, Star went to the door. Cade's truck came up the driveway. She frowned. Terrific, what did he want—a repeat of last night's kiss? No way. She was not her mother, ready and available for any guy that just happened to come along. A giant chip on her shoulder, Star met Cade at the door.

He came up the porch steps, a casserole dish in his hands. "Your mother sent you dinner. It's chicken enchiladas."

Surprised, Star took the warm dish from him. "Really?" Her bravado faded. "My mom isn't the greatest cook, but she does make decent enchiladas. Thanks, I'm starving."

Cade followed her inside. Star snagged a plate from the rack near the sink.

"She sent enough for two," Cade said. "Mind if I join you?"

"You haven't eaten yet?" Star asked. She took a second plate from the rack.

"I was going to, then your mother sent me here." He smiled. "She's not very subtle."

Star shook her head. "No, she's not. Have a seat." She set the plates on the table. The spicy scent of chicken and chili sauce filled the air. "Diet soda or wine?" she offered. "That's all I have."

"Soda." Cade sat.

Star returned with two cans of soda then took a seat. "You're a lifesaver. I was just about to make myself a cheese omelet for dinner. Boring."

Cade forked up some enchilada. "This is great."

"Um hum," Star agreed, her own mouth full.

They ate in companionable silence, and it seemed easy between them for once. No agenda. Just two hungry people enjoying a good meal.

"How's Trudy?" Star asked between bites.

"Fine. Resting." Cade chewed, his expression thoughtful. "Your mom's doing a good job."

"When do John and Ernie leave?" She had no desire to bear witness to another late night sex fest.

"Not until Saturday. They booked the full week."

Star's hopes sank. "That long, huh?"

"Why?" Cade asked. "Is there a problem?"

"No," she said a bit too quickly. She wasn't going to rat her mother out, no matter how much she disapproved of her actions.

Cade finished his enchilada and took a long drink of soda. "I'm stuffed."

"Me, too." She stood. "Let me wash the dish so you can take it back."

"Sit down." Cade gestured to her chair. "I don't think your food's even hit your stomach yet."

"Oh." Star lowered herself back onto the chair. "I thought you'd want to get home."

"Why?" He leaned back, looking entirely too male to suit her.

"The kids? The guests?" she said, reminding him of his life.

"Ron's covering for me."

"I see." He stared at her, the hungry look back in his eyes. Her mind screamed danger, yet she didn't move.

"Any interest in seeing a movie? They're showing *Yours, Mine and Ours*, the original, at the park tonight."

"They still do that?" Star had loved the outdoor movies when she'd been a kid. They'd always gone. A free event was not something her family passed up.

"Every Sunday night during the summer."

She looked hard at Cade, not sure how to take his

invitation. "I don't know."

"It's just a movie, Star," he said, as if reading her mind. "In a public place."

What could happen? "Okay, I'll go. I'm a sucker for Lucille Ball." This time when she stood, he didn't protest. He rose, too, taking his own plate to the sink. Star washed the dishes, and Cade dried. Again, it was too easy between them, and more alarm bells sounded, but Star ignored the warnings and went to freshen up.

Quickly, she showered, dressing in jeans and a simple white T-shirt edged at the neck with pretty lace. She slid her feet into her turquoise flip flops with the monkeys on the soles, and grabbed a thick blue hooded sweatshirt. The nights here were cool, and she knew she'd need the jacket later.

She found Cade on the porch, sitting on the top step, the can of soda in his hands.

"That was fast," he said when he saw her. Then, "You're beautiful."

The compliment heated her skin, and made it even harder for her to think about keeping him at arm's length. "I feel better now that I don't smell like baby spit up."

"I'll take you any way I can get you, Starlene White."

Desire curled low in her belly. He was doing it again, seducing her with sweet words.

"Don't, Cade," she said, tamping down the confusion his compliment stirred. The way he looked at her, as if she were the only woman for him, made her want to give in to him, to the romance he promised, yet she couldn't let go. Not with him. "Let's just go to the movie, okay?"

* * *

It didn't get dark in Seward until nearly daybreak this time of year, but that didn't stop the town from showing the outdoor movie.

A covered area in the park was darkened on three sides with black cloth. The movie screen was inset and surprisingly easy to see, even in the muted daylight. Although they'd arrived about thirty minutes early, the lawn was already covered with several blankets and low riding lawn chairs.

"Is this a good spot?" Cade asked when they found a vacant patch of grass.

"Works for me," Star replied.

Cade spread the blanket out on the grass. There was a good turnout tonight, probably around seventy people. Star recognized some of them: the gal from the diner, one of the nurses from the hospital, and a checker from the local store.

Cade knew everyone, and they'd stopped several times to greet people while making their way through the crowd. To Star's surprise, a lot of people remembered her and a part of her liked that, liked being a part of a community. Her life in Seattle didn't allow time for things like neighbors, and she certainly didn't know anyone there from her childhood.

"Have a seat," Cade said.

Star lowered herself to the blanket. "What do you have in that bag?"

Cade grinned as he dropped down beside her. He reached in the bag and pulled out a bottle of wine.

"Wine? Is that legal?"

"It is if you don't get caught." He smiled before fishing a bag of pre-popped popcorn from the sack.

"Popcorn?"

Next came a box of Milk Duds.

"Are you kidding?" Star asked. "Wine, popcorn, and Milk Duds are a strange combo. You brought a lot of snacks when you couldn't be sure I'd agree to this."

"A guy can always hope." Cade's smile deepened.

Star shook her head, unable to resist his charm.

"Besides," Cade said, "you haven't lived until you've had Milk Duds and popcorn mixed together. We need the wine to wash it all down." He opened the box of candy and shook the contents into the bag of popcorn. "Try some." He held the bag out to her.

Skeptical, Star tried a handful. The chocolate and caramel mixed with the salty popcorn. She smiled. "This is good. Like caramel corn."

"Told you. It's even better when the popcorn is hot." Cade removed the cork from the wine and filled two clear plastic cups, passing one to Star. "Cheers."

Star touched her glass to his. "Cheers."

"Let's drink to the first day of the rest of our lives."

"Cheesy, O'Brien," Star said. "But okay. To the rest of our lives." They touched glasses again. Star took a sip of wine. "This is good, too."

"Merlot. To go with the chocolate."

Star smiled.

"How much longer are you in town?" He tossed a handful of popcorn into his mouth.

"One week. I leave next Sunday."

Cade frowned. "Not long then."

"Nope." Star sipped her wine. "I wouldn't stay on this long, but I promised Brandi I'd hang out for a while." Star inhaled. The scented air overwhelmed her, the hemlock, the stink of the fish from the bay, and the wild fireweed. "I'm going to miss the air here."

"Just the air?" Cade teased.

"And Brandi and Will," she joked.

"Will you miss me, Star?" His serious tone caught her off guard.

"I think so," she replied honestly. "If you'd asked me that question last week I would have said, no, but now you're starting to grow on me a little. Plus, you made me this delicious popcorn. That will earn you some serious points in my book."

He chuckled, his laugh breaking the serious moment.

People continued to arrive. Soon the lawn was totally covered with bright blankets. Whole families had come, and their laughter filled the park. Children played. Neighbors visited.

Star glanced at Cade and found him watching her. "We should have brought the kids."

"Then it wouldn't be a date." Cade reclined, rolling to his

side, propping his torso up on his elbow.

"It's not a date."

"If you say so."

"I'm not used to you being nice to me," she said. "I keep waiting for the other shoe to drop."

"The shoe's not going to drop." He took a sip of his wine and appeared to be considering her words. "I always wanted to be nice to you, even when I was awful. And later, when we were teenagers, I didn't know how to fix all the things I'd done."

"I guess I can understand where you were coming from, now that I know about Patsy and your dad. I'm sorry their relationship was so hard on you. I guess I don't know how I would have reacted had I known about them."

"I'm over it."

"I know. Tell me about your wife," she asked, wondering how much, if anything, he'd share with her. "What was she like?"

He sat back up. "That would depend on the day."

"What do you mean?"

"Marissa was extremely bipolar. She was up. She was down. When she was up, life was great. When she was down, she was suicidal and needed constant supervision."

"Wow, she sounds a lot like my mom," Star said. "I've always thought my mom was bipolar, but when I suggested as much to her, she read me the riot act. I can't imagine what you and the kids went through."

Cade reached over and squeezed her hand. "I didn't realize about Destiny."

Star shrugged. "We survived her. Tell me more about Marissa."

"Because of her illness, we'd agreed not to have any more children after Brad, but Marissa became pregnant with the twins." Cade looked up at the sky, and Star knew the memories played in his head. "I always wanted a big family, lots of kids.

"Her illness was rough on all of us," he said. "She hated it here. She wanted to live in the city, in Seattle or L.A. She begged me to take her out of this town, but my life was here and will always be here."

"She died in a car accident, is that right?" Star prompted.

He nodded. "I'd finally talked her into getting some help. She was due to leave the following Monday for Seattle, but I don't believe she ever had any intention of going. That day, she'd wanted to keep Brad home from school, but he wasn't sick, so I made him go. The second I was gone, she loaded up the twins. The police said she didn't even brake when she drove into the lake. She wanted to take the kids with her." Remembered pain creased his forehead. "How can a mother do that, Star? I mean, her own kids?"

Star didn't have an answer for him, but the agony in his voice twisted her own heart. "How did Finn and Emma get out of the car?"

"There was a witness to the accident. He dove in and pulled the kids out. Finn had a broken arm. Emma, some bruises. When he went back for Marissa, he couldn't find her. They recovered her body later that afternoon. I've spent a lot of time beating myself up. I should have watched her better, but she seemed fine that day. In the end, I couldn't have stopped her. She'd have found a way to take her own life."

"And Brad?" Star asked. "How has the accident affected him?"

"He's angry. He blames me for making him go to school. He thinks he could have stopped her if he'd been with her that day. And maybe he could have, I don't know. I've tried to explain to Brad about Marissa's mental condition, and I think he understands now, but she broke his heart."

"That's awful. Her story is so tragic."

"The kids suffered the most," Cade said. "They've had extensive counseling. Finn recently quit having nightmares. Emma handled it better; I'm not sure why. It was a blessing when Ron and Trudy moved in with us. Trudy especially. The kids need a woman in their lives."

Overcome with compassion, Star placed her hand over

Cade's. His hand shifted and he laced his fingers with hers, holding on, as if she were some kind of lifeline for him, and something inside Star softened.

"I don't want to talk about Marissa anymore." His attention focused totally on Star.

"Me either."

His fingers tightened around hers, and a bond formed between them. He'd trusted her with his past, and that trust honored her, made her want to smooth away all his hurts, all the pain he'd endured.

The movie began. Music filled the air, the happy notes chasing away the melancholy silence between them.

"Popcorn?" Cade asked as he came back to a sitting position on the blanket.

"Yes, please."

They watched the movie, munched popcorn, drank wine, and most importantly, they laughed, the laughter chasing away the ghosts of their pasts.

When the movie ended, they stayed where they were, mellow and sated, in no hurry to leave. All around them, people packed up their blankets and left.

For the first time in her life, Star didn't want the day to end. She knew she'd stay up all night with Cade if he wanted her to. She didn't want to break this new connection between them.

Cade moved to his back, his hands cradled under his head.

Star copied him. The sky was not quite blue and not quite white, but more lavender. A twilight sky.

Cade turned his head to look at her. Star did the same. Their faces only inches apart.

"I had a good time tonight," Star said.

"I don't want to take you home yet."

"Okay."

Cade stroked her cheek. "You've always been the prettiest girl in Seward." His fingers trailed over her jaw, to her neck. "I always hoped you'd come back. I wanted the chance to set things right with you."

His words made her tingle—all over, and heaven help her, she liked the sensation.

Cade's fingers moved through her hair, lifting the strands then letting them fall. On their sides, they faced each other now. Star could barely think with him so close. She loved his mouth, the sensuous curve of his upper lip. He had great lips. Strong lips. She wanted him to kiss her. She didn't care if they were in the middle of a public park. What did it matter? She wasn't staying on. She had nothing to lose except her pride, and who would know once she was back in Seattle?

Cade's lips parted slightly.

Unable to resist, she kissed him.

He moaned, low, the sound better than any words would have been. She may have started the kiss, but Cade took over, taking Star onto her back. His mouth worked magic on hers. She forgot everything but him. If this was a dream she never wanted to wake up.

The kiss went on and on, sending Star deeper and deeper into a state of arousal she'd never experienced before. Her body grew weightless and heavy at the same time. His hands slipped inside her sweatshirt jacket, under her T-shirt, to her back. His rough palms stroked her sensitive skin.

"We need to get out of here," Cade whispered in her ear. "Now, or I'm going to make love to you here. In public."

The words hit her like ice water. Star's eyes snapped open. Good grief, she was just like her mother—wanton to the core! Quickly, she scanned the area. Only one other couple remained, and they were involved in their own necking.

Embarrassed, Star sat up and pulled her T-shirt back down into place.

"I'm sorry," she said. "I don't know what happened."

Cade sat up, then gave her a cocky smile. "You don't know what happened?"

Star pursed her lips. "I know what happened; I just don't know why I let it."

"Some things you just can't control." Cade touched her face, gently, sweetly.

On the verge of kissing him again, Star pushed to her knees. "We should go."

He reached for her again, the predatory glow back in his eyes.

"No, I mean it." She stood. She might be prone to sex thanks to her mother, but she didn't need to perform in public.

Cade sighed, obviously disappointed. Without looking at her, he packed up the bag, stuffing the blanket inside.

Star moved away. She'd never suspected she could lose control like that and the knowledge unsettled her. She loved control, fed on it. She needed time to think, to sort out these new, strong feelings.

"I don't suppose you want to take this back to your place?" Cade asked, sounding hopeful.

"I'm sure my mom's there," she hedged, more afraid to confront her own sexuality than she wanted to admit.

"Then let's go somewhere else."

She couldn't look at him. "I can't."

"Why?"

She knew he didn't understand, but she had no intention of telling him she was a frightened virgin. And she wasn't just scared of the sex, or of her own powerful reaction to him. She was afraid Cade would break her heart.

"Don't run away, Star," Cade said. "Take a chance."

"I can't. Not yet." Regret heavy in her chest, Star walked away. When she reached his truck, she got inside. Cade didn't speak on the ride back to Patsy's. Relief filled her when she saw Brandi's car in the driveway. Her mother was home.

Star opened the door of the truck. "Thanks for tonight."

"Star."

Star jumped from the truck. She didn't want to hear what he had to say, couldn't take any more pressure from him.

Cade had given her a taste of sex tonight.

Heaven help her, she wanted more.

At the door, Star twisted the knob. At the same time her mother yanked the door open from the inside.

"Star," Destiny cried. "Come quick. I think I've killed John."

CHAPTER ELEVEN

"What?" Star took in her mother's disheveled appearance: the bed-head, the short black robe. "John's here? Again?"

"In the bedroom." Destiny grabbed Star's arm. "He needs help."

"Wait," Star said, remembering Cade. She turned, relieved to find him still sitting in the driveway. Star waved Cade in before following her mother to the bedroom.

"I think John's having a heart attack," Destiny said in a rush. "We were, well, you know, and he suddenly stopped. He's clutching his chest."

Star found John in the bedroom, flat on his back, the sheet twisted about his hips. The stench of booze and sweat gagged Star.

"John, what's happening?" Star asked.

"A pain." He squeezed his eyes shut. "My chest. Get aspirin."

Star spun from the room, nearly running into Cade in the hall.

"What's going on?" Cade asked.

"It's John," Star said. "Possible heart attack."

"John?" Cade shook his head, heading for the bedroom.

In the medicine cabinet Star found a bottle of generic aspirin. She heard Cade asking John questions. She raced back to John with the pills. Fingers shaking, she shook out a tablet.

"Under my tongue." John opened his mouth. Star placed the tablet inside.

"Destiny," Cade called over his shoulder. "Take my truck. Go to the house and call 911."

For a second Destiny didn't move. Star said, "Go, Mom." Destiny ran from the room. The front door banged shut.

"How can I help?" Star asked Cade.

"Let the aspirin work," John said.

Star wracked her brain, trying to remember the one CPR/First Aid class she'd had.

"Hang on," Cade said, the voice of reason. "Help will be here soon."

"We're in the middle of nowhere," John said, his words sounding more like a wheeze than actual words.

"It'll be okay," Cade told him. "Try not to worry. Relax."

But in the back of Star's mind she saw Patsy having her own heart attack. She hadn't survived. Would John?

Sweat beaded John's brow, his upper lip. Star retrieved a dry washcloth from the bathroom. She blotted the moisture from his face.

"Is the pain any better?" Cade asked.

"Some."

"Hang on, John," Star said. "Mom's sure to be at Cade's by now. Help is on the way. An aid car can make it here in minutes."

He nodded, clearly too spent to argue with her.

"Everything's going to be fine," she droned on, not sure what else to say. She exchanged a concerned look with Cade. Thank God, Cade was here. Silently, Star prayed that John would live, that he'd be okay. Destiny would never recover if she thought her sexual prowess had killed a man.

After what seemed like an eternity, she heard the slam of a car door. Destiny was back.

"Help's coming," her mother called out.

To Star's untrained eye, John looked better. His face

wasn't as pinched, and he didn't seem to be sweating as much. Had the aspirin worked?

From outside the faint whine of a siren cut through the night.

"Here they come," Star said. "I'll go and flag them down."

"Thanks, Star," Cade said, a long look passing between them.

Star ran from the room. Her mother sat on the couch, Star's blanket wrapped around her body, Destiny's pretty face, ravaged by tears. Star barely spared a glance for her mother as she flipped on the outdoor lights and went outside. An aid vehicle came toward her, the red light spitting color everywhere. The shrill siren knotted her stomach. She met the EMTs in the driveway.

"He's inside," she said. "Follow me."

The men, both clean cut and young, probably in their late twenties, grabbed their gear and followed Star inside.

"Is he still responsive?" one of the men asked.

"Yes," she said. "He's talking to us."

Star and the EMTs blew by Destiny. Like Star, the men barely glanced at her mother. When they reached the bedroom, one of the men said, "Wait here."

Star did as she was told. She hovered in the hallway. She could hear the men talking to Cade, asking more questions. Star wrapped her arms around herself. A chill invaded her body. The hairs on the back of her neck stood up.

A minute later, Cade joined her. "You okay?"

She nodded. "Just cold."

"Son of a—" Cade raked his fingers through his hair, and Star realized he felt as emotionally charged as she did.

"Yeah," Star said, totally getting it.

Cade reached for her, gathering her to his chest. The wall inside Star crumbled and she melted into him. Her arms wrapped around him. They held each other, and funny, some of her anxiety dissolved.

Minutes later, one of the EMTs stepped out into the hall.

"He's stable," the man said. "We're going to transport

him."

"Okay," Cade said. "I'll be right behind you."

Star turned at the sound of Ernie's voice. "What's going on?" he shouted at Destiny. "What did you do?"

Her mother burst into tears.

"Cade," Ernie said when he saw them. "Is he okay?"

"Yes." Cade walked to meet Ernie. "He's stable. They're getting ready to transport him to the hospital."

Ernie turned to Destiny, but thankfully, no words came out of his mouth.

"This is my fault," Destiny said between sobs.

"Get a grip, Mom," Star said. "This could have happened to him anywhere, with anyone."

"But he was so...energetic," Destiny said.

Star groaned. "Mom, stop talking."

"I'll second that," Cade said.

One of the EMTs brought a gurney into the bedroom. Soon after, John was wheeled out.

"John," Destiny cried when she saw him. "I'm so sorry."

John gave her a thumbs up.

"Do you want me to come with you?" Destiny asked.

"Yes," John said.

Destiny nodded. "I'll get dressed and follow the ambulance." She gave Star a smile before leaving them.

In a matter of minutes, the ambulance was gone. Ernie and Destiny pulled out after it.

On shaky legs, Star followed Cade down the steps.

"Will you be all right here?" he asked.

Star glanced back at the mobile home. She had no desire to go back inside. "I'll be fine."

"Why don't you stay at my place? We have the room." He opened the door of his truck.

"No, I'm okay."

He frowned. "You're not fine, Star. Go to my place. Ron is up. Tell him I said to put you in the copper room. I'll let your mother know where you are."

Star eyed the mobile home. She really did not want to go

back inside. Not tonight. The thought of being near other people: Trudy, Ron, and even the kids, sounded comforting.

"Okay, I'll go."

He smiled. "Good. I'll see you there later."

Star didn't wait for him to drive away. Instead, she went inside and packed a small bag. She needed people. Cade's people.

* * *

Star focused on the bright morning light streaming through the window of Cade's guest room. A manly room, with a copper colored bedspread done in a fish print. One wall held a large metal fish, the other a painting of the Kenai River.

She checked her watch. It was after eight. Breakfast was probably already over and done with. She needed to get up and get down there, but the events of last night reeled through Star's head, her mother meeting her at the door, the paramedics, Cade. Star burrowed deeper under the covers.

She closed her eyes against the morning glare, against the harsh reality of her life. How would she ever face Cade or any of the O'Briens this morning? It had been bad enough answering Ron's questions last night. Her mother's sexual prowess had almost killed one of their guests.

Death couldn't be good for business.

The bedroom door creaked. "Star?" Finn's head poked into the room.

"Hey, Finn." She smiled at the little boy, who had a serious case of bed-head.

"Dad says to come down. Breakfast is ready."

"Thanks. I'll be right down."

He disappeared from view.

With the opening of the bedroom door came the scent of pancakes and bacon. Star ignored her embarrassment and got out of bed. She took the robe provided for guests from a hook on the back of the door and slipped it on, belting it around her waist.

106

On bare feet, she walked down the stairs to the kitchen.

Finn, Emma, and Brad sat at the table eating. Cade stood at the counter, flipping pancakes.

"Morning," he said when he saw her. For a second he searched her face, and when she smiled at him, he smiled back.

"Good morning," she said. "How's John?"

"Resting comfortably," Cade said. "He's stable. They're calling it a cardiac episode, not an actual heart attack. That's good news. He'll be having some additional tests today. I know this might come as a shock, but your mother is a pretty good nurse. She's been a real advocate for John."

"Is Ernie still there, too?" Star asked.

"Yes. He wanted to stay."

"Of course."

"Grab a plate," Cade said, "then come here."

Star snagged an empty plate from the table and walked to Cade. This was normal, breakfast with your family. So why did it feel so foreign?

He loaded her plate with three pancakes, two pieces of bacon, and a fried egg.

"Wait," she said. "My life doesn't revolve around meals in Seattle. I can't eat all of this."

He winked at her. "Sure you can. Meals are a time when families come together. Get used to it, Star."

Star gave up and took her plate to the table, taking the seat opposite Brad. She did feel like part of the family here, but how much would she miss these people when she left?

"Here." Finn passed her the syrup.

Cade set his own plate on the table and sat.

For a few minutes they all ate in silence—like they were a real family. What would that be like? She looked around the table. The kids. Cade. Whoa, wait a minute. She wasn't anybody's mother, and she didn't want to be. Being Cade's potential lover, okay, but not a mother. No way. She wasn't about to get stuck in this town. The thought killed her appetite and she pushed her plate away.

"You okay?" Cade wiped his mouth on his napkin.

"No." Star finished her coffee. "I'm so sorry about what happened last night."

"It wasn't your fault." Cade frowned. "Don't apologize for her."

"I'm not."

"You are," Cade said. "Destiny and John made their own choice. Just like you and I make our own choices. Just like my father made his own choices."

"Wait, what happened exactly?" Brad asked, his mouth full of pancakes.

"You know what happened." Cade stood and began clearing the plates.

Thankfully, Brad let his question drop.

Star got up to help, Cade's words rattling around in her head. What choice did she want to make with regard to Cade? Could she have her summer fling and move on? Any good Cosmo girl would.

Together they cleaned the kitchen. Finn and Emma wandered in with Snowbell.

"It's a rare day off for us," Cade said. "No guests."

Star winced. "Sorry."

"What I mean is," Cade said, "we should do something fun."

"Like what?" Emma asked with interest.

"What about a hike? Or a bike ride?" Cade suggested.

"Okay." Finn jumped up and down.

"Star has to come," Emma said. "You'll come, won't you, Star?"

"I don't think so," Star said. "I have some work to finish up."

"Take the day off," Cade said softly. "Spend it with me, with us. It's one day out of your life, Star."

"But Mom," Star began.

"Can take care of herself. I don't see her leaving John's side anytime soon."

Star's teeth grazed her lower lip. "I don't know." It wasn't her work that kept her from saying yes; it was the O'Briens. In her heart she knew that the more time she spent with them, the more time she'd have to become attached.

"Please, Star," Emma begged. "Please, please, please."

"Oh, all right." Deep down, she wanted to go, wanted to be included. "Can we hike up to the top of Eagle Ridge?"

Cade traded glances with the twins. "I don't see why not."

Star grinned. "I'll go and get dressed."

"Hurry, Star," Emma said, her eyes bright with excitement. Star touched the little girl's hair. "I will."

"Come on." Finn tugged on her hand. The little boy pulled her to the stairs, leading her to her room. "Now hurry."

He left Star at her door.

Star had no choice but to go inside and dress. She grabbed the change of clothes she'd brought and headed for the bathroom.

She had to admit, she loved the idea of the hike. Since coming back to Alaska she'd had very little time for sightseeing. She'd earned this day out.

Humming, Star stepped into the shower.

CHAPTER TWELVE

Star winced.

"You okay?" Cade offered her his hand, ready to help her down yet another steep incline.

The hike to the top of Eagle Ridge was everything Star remembered. The scents of the forest combined with the way the sunlight filtered down through the canopy of branches and emerald leaves overhead lent an enchantment to the hike. Wild daisies and fireweed grew with abandon, adding bright spots of color. This was nature at its finest, raw and unspoiled.

And although her feet ached something awful, she didn't want to stop.

"I'm fine." She took his hand, but she must have winced again because he said, "You're not fine. Is it the boots?"

She'd borrowed some hiking boots from the collection Cade kept for the guests. At first, the boots had felt fine; now the darn things were biting into her feet in a number of places.

"Wait up," Cade called to the kids.

Down the path, Finn, Emma, and Brad stopped, turning to stare at them. All three looked as tired and hot as Star felt.

"Sit down." Cade helped her to a nearby fallen long.

When she was seated, he unlaced the boot.

"I don't think you should take it off," Star said. "I'll never get it back on."

"I have some moleskin in my first aid kit. If we work quickly we should be able to get the boot back on before your foot swells."

"Great," Star said dryly.

Cade eased the boot from her foot. Blood dotted her sock. Cade frowned. "Why didn't you say something sooner?"

Star shrugged. "I didn't want to be a crybaby."

With a shake of his head, Cade removed the other boot, then took the first aid kit from his backpack. Cool fingers eased her bloodied socks off. He tore open a package, producing an antiseptic pad, and cleaned the sores, his touch gentle.

"Ow," Star cried when the antiseptic met raw skin.

"Sorry." He covered the sores with the moleskin before putting her socks back on, his fingers lingering on her ankle a little longer than necessary. Star loved the way his fingers felt against her skin. It was almost worth the blisters to have him touch her.

Her injured feet fought with the boots, but Cade managed to get the boots back on without dislodging the moleskin.

"Thanks," she said.

His eyes met hers. "You're welcome."

Star stared into his eyes, wanted to drown in the crystal blueness. In his eyes she saw his want, his need for her. He didn't attempt to hide his emotions, and the intensity both thrilled and frightened her.

Finn and Emma had wandered back to them, taking a seat on either side of Star, breaking the sexual current that seemed to pass between her and Cade each time they were close.

Brad remained up-trail, sprawled out on another fallen log. He hadn't wanted to go hiking with them and had spent most of the day sulking.

Star exchanged a look with Emma. The little girl shook her head sadly.

"Okay," Cade said. "Let's get you up." He pulled Star to

her feet. "How do you feel?" He kept his hands locked around her forearms, steadying her.

Star tested her weight on her feet. "Better. Thanks."

Cade took her arm. "Let's go. We're almost there."

Each step Star took felt like fire, even with the moleskin on, but she ignored her pain and kept walking. A definite limp accompanied her steps.

Cade kept pace with her, his arm going around her for support. They walked together, almost as one, their sides bumping. Star's internal inferno rose and kept rising.

"Stop," Cade said.

"Why?" She wanted to reach the end of the trail as quickly as possible and put an end to whatever it was that was happening between them.

"Put your arms around my neck." Cade held his arms out to her.

"Excuse me?"

"Do it, Star."

Realization dawned. He wanted to carry her. "No way, O'Brien. I can make it."

He came at her, lifting Star off her feet, leaving her no choice but to throw her arms around his neck.

"Put me down." His face was too close to hers, his arms too intimate around her. To her distress, her long dormant hormones roared to life and she prayed he couldn't hear the rapid tempo of her heart.

"It's only a quarter of a mile more." He started forward.

"I'm too heavy."

"No, you're not." Cade charged ahead. "You don't weigh anything at all."

Star had no choice but to let him carry her. And in truth, it felt wonderful to take the weight off her aching feet. Beyond them, the kids walked, Finn and Emma pausing every now and again to admire a bird or a pretty flower. The heady scent of earth and warmed spruce and wild berries filled Star's head. But it was Cade's scent that nearly did her in. He smelled of fresh air and sweat and something else, fabric softener? The combination put butterflies in Star's stomach. His hair tickled the back of her hand and she resisted the urge to let her fingers creep up into the softness.

"Relax," he whispered, his lips near her ear, the word a caress on her skin.

How could she? Her body tensed. She couldn't relax. She couldn't draw air.

When they exited the path, Star sighed. She didn't miss Cade's amused smile. The twins and Brad waited at the truck.

Cade set her down, and Star used him to steady herself. "Thank you."

Cade grinned. "My pleasure."

For a second they didn't move, then Emma said, "Open the truck, Dad."

Cade glanced away. He let the kids into the truck before helping Star into the passenger seat, passing each of them a cold bottle of water. They made the ride home in silence. Finn slept, soft snores coming from his slack mouth. Emma's head leaned against the window, then she too, slept. Brad's eyes were closed, his ear buds in his ears, his iPod cranked up.

The hum of the engine relaxed Star. She let the purr pull her under and the next thing she knew they were in the O'Briens' driveway.

Cade cut the engine.

Brad exited the truck, the action waking Finn and Emma. The little girl yawned.

Cade helped the kids out of the truck.

Star opened her own door.

Cade rounded the truck. "Scoot to me."

"I can walk to the house." Star swiveled her legs toward the open truck door. "My feet aren't that bad."

Brad, Emma, and Finn headed for the house. All three kids looked as wiped out as Star felt. Hiking, while fun, was exercise, and she'd had more than her share today. She ached all over but in a good way.

"I disagree," Cade said. "I saw the way you were limping. You should have said something sooner. Because you didn't, we're doing things my way now."

He scooped her from the truck, leaving Star no choice but to hang on. Once inside, he set her on the couch in the family room.

"Wait here," he ordered with a stern look.

Star wanted to protest but kept her mouth shut. What good would it do? She wouldn't win against Cade. He was a man on a mission, and his mission was to take care of her feet.

At the sound of Ron's voice, Star's ears perked up.

"Any update?" Cade asked his brother.

"John had the tests. They've released him. Destiny is on her way back here."

"That's good news," Cade said.

"Sounds like it."

"Trudy?"

"She's good," Ron said. "We had a relaxing day. How was the hike?"

"Great, but Star's feet are pretty torn up."

"That's not good," Ron said with sympathy. "City feet."

"Yeah," Cade agreed.

The men moved out of earshot. Star bent and removed her borrowed boots and bloody socks. She grimaced. Two red, raw sores marred her heels. She'd never admit to Cade that her heels had already been damaged when she'd walked home from his place her first day in Seward. Now it would be days before she could wear real shoes again. Thank goodness for flip flops.

Cade returned with a dishpan full of steaming water.

"I don't know," Star said skeptically. "That hot water looks painful."

He set the pan at her feet. "You'll feel better after you soak." He kneeled at her feet, his hands closing around them, his touch gentle. Her feet in his hands, he slid them into the water.

The warm water stung at first but quickly began to ease some of the ache.

"Soak," he said. "I'll be back."

Star watched him walk away, her gaze sliding across his broad shoulders, down his strong back, and lower, to his rear end. When she realized she was practically drooling, she gave herself a mental check.

Yet, a nagging voice said, you want him. Use him. Make him your first. Be a modern girl. It's just sex. Her mother had sex all the time. Brandi had sex. Tawney and Ruby Sue had sex. Everyone but her had sex.

She wanted to have sex with Cade. She couldn't deny her urges any longer. For the first time she wanted to understand what the fuss was all about. If she made love with him, she'd have to live with the consequences. She'd return to her life and leave him behind.

In fact, he'd be the perfect partner, no strings attached. He'd become a memory, albeit, a great one. She could do it, because the alternative would be to leave here without sleeping with him, and that was a choice she didn't want to make. Better to give herself to him, than to walk away and never know the joy of spending the night in his arms.

"How do you feel now?" Cade asked, snapping her out of her musings.

"Better." She smiled, the choice clear in her mind. Loving Cade, even for one night, was worth the risk to her heart.

Cade grinned back. Star heated all over.

All over.

* * *

"It was awful, Star. Just awful."

Star took a sip of her ice tea and exchanged an exasperated look with Cade before replying, "He's on the mend now, Mom. Let it go."

Destiny shook her head. "I can't. I feel so responsible. I could have killed him. I had no idea I was that good in bed."

Beside her, Cade made a funny sound and Star felt sure he was biting back a full-out belly laugh.

"Have some more wine." Star refilled her mother's glass.

They sat around the outdoor table on the O'Briens' back patio, enjoying the warm evening. Trudy sat nearby in her lounge chair, Ron beside her in a deck chair. The kids had gone inside, leaving the grownups alone to rehash the past twenty-four hours.

It had rained earlier, and the air smelled twice as sweet as usual. Star inhaled deeply, wanting to remember the scents, knowing she'd go back over this day a million times once she was back in Seattle.

Destiny chugged her wine. "I'm a wreck."

"You've been through a lot," Trudy said with sympathy.

"John was glad you were there," Ron added.

"Yes, he was." Destiny smiled. "He told me so over and over again. He's asked me to come home with him, you know."

Star choked, coughing. They all knew. This was the third time Destiny had delivered the news. She tuned out her mother and mentally counted the days she had left in Seward; Tuesday, Wednesday, Thursday, Friday, Saturday, fly home Sunday. Six more nights. She could do it. She could make it.

"Want to take a walk?" Under the table, Cade's hand found hers.

She gave him a grateful smile. "I'd love to."

Destiny kept talking, and for a moment, Star felt bad leaving Trudy and Ron with her mother, but Cade took her elbow and guided her from the patio. Her feet felt better now, able to stretch and relax in her flip flops.

As they walked away, Star missed the darkness that night brought in Seattle. She longed to be swallowed up in the shadows, longed for the privacy a dark evening would give them. The never-ending daylight left them exposed and part of everything going on around them. Now that she'd made the decision to sleep with Cade, she wanted to be alone with him.

"Come on." Cade led her around the corner of the garage, to the side door. He opened the door and pulled her inside.

"What are we—" before she could finish her question, he

kicked the door closed, and then he was kissing her, delivering one mind blowing kiss after another.

Star's thoughts scrambled. In the semi-darkness, her fingers curled into the front of his T-shirt and she held on for dear life. The scent of damp earth and man fueled her.

"I've wanted to kiss you all day," Cade said between kisses. He nibbled at her lip, her jaw, kissed the pulse point on her neck. "I give up, Star. I can't stay away from you. Don't push me away this time."

Star's back met the side of the garage. Cade leaned against her, pressed against her, rubbed against her.

"Meet me tonight," Cade whispered against her mouth, his voice raw with need.

"Where?"

"I don't know," he said. "My bedroom?"

"Too risky."

"Right." He kissed her again. "The walls are thin."

Star's eyes popped open a little wider at that remark.

"Patsy's?" he asked.

"No. Yuck."

He smiled against her mouth. "I don't care where, Star."

"What about here?" Star asked. It was dark, private.

"The garage?" Cade shook his head. "No. I want to make a memory."

His hands crept under her shirt, up to her bra. With one hand, Cade unhooked the strap.

Star gave a low gasp.

"Eagle Ridge? The parking lot at the bottom of the ridge. Should be empty at night."

"What?" Star asked, losing her train of thought as his hands came around and slipped under her bra to cup her breasts. Her eyes slid shut.

"Eagle Ridge?" he repeated, his fingers finding her nipples.

"Okay." At this moment, she didn't care where they met, so long as they did.

"It's private," Cade said.

"Yes," she whispered.

He captured her mouth.

Star kissed him back. She wanted more. She wanted him, all of him. He was unfinished business, that was all. After tonight, she could return home and get on with the rest of her life.

Cade released her breasts and brought his hands to her hips, pulling her tight against him. The hard shaft of his arousal pressed against her belly.

Outside the garage, Destiny's laughter pierced the air.

"We should get back," Star said. "Mom's drunk."

Cade sighed. "Put her to bed. I'll put the kids to bed then meet you downstairs."

Star nodded.

Cade kissed her hard and long before letting her go. Like an expert, he refastened her bra.

Together they left the garage, both of them aching with need, both of them craving release.

* * *

Star pulled the covers up over Destiny. Her mother hiccupped. Star smoothed her mother's hair back from her forehead. She'd been unable to talk Destiny into washing her face. Black mascara ringed her mother's eyes, stained her cheeks. Tonight, Destiny looked faded, older, not as bright and shiny as she once had been. Sadness settled in Star's heart. She didn't want to wind up like her mother, alone and the object of pity.

"I can't do it," Destiny said, her eyes on Star.

"Do what, Mom?"

"Be a nurse to him."

Star glanced at her mother. "To John?"

Destiny shook her head. "I don't want an invalid for a husband."

"You're not marrying him, Mom," Star reminded her. "You just met the guy."

"He's expecting me to move to Canada. To play nursemaid."

"So tell him you've changed your mind," Star said. "He'll understand. He barely knows you. If he did, he'd know you're not nurse material. Besides, I don't think he needs a nurse. He's going to be fine."

Tears filled Destiny's eyes. "I've screwed up again, haven't I, baby?"

Star sighed. She'd heard it all before, the self-pity, the apology that came whenever her mother broke up with another man.

"No, Mom." Star geared up for her usual pep talk. "You're right to step back. Absolutely right."

Destiny smiled. "Really, baby?"

"Really. Now go to sleep. Everything will be better tomorrow."

"Promise?"

"I do." Star crossed her heart. "Now, sleep."

Destiny snuggled under the covers. Star sat with her mom until soft snores came, slow and steady.

Some things never changed. She was still the mother and Destiny was still her child. The thought saddened her and brought on a melancholy she wished she could shake off.

A soft knock sounded on their door. Star left the bed and opened the door.

"Everything okay?" Cade asked, but his eyes said, come with me. I want you.

Star glanced at her mother. "I should stay with Mom. She's a mess."

"Live your own life, Star." He touched her cheek, his touch tender. "Destiny will land on her feet. She always does. Come with me."

A painful longing squeezed her chest. "I don't know."

Cade took her hand, giving it a tug. "Come on, Star. Come out and play." He smiled.

Star caved. "Okay."

Cade pulled her into the hall and closed the door.

"Are the twins asleep?" Star asked.

"You just can't help being responsible, can you?" Cade

asked with wonder. "The kids are fine. Ron will keep an ear open for them and for Brad."

Cade was right. She was responsible to a fault. For once, she wanted to be the irresponsible one. What did irresponsibility feel like? Was it liberating?

Cade tugged her down the stairs and out the front door. They ran all the way to the truck. Star giggled, feeling like a teenager, like being with Cade was forbidden.

Once in the truck, Cade did a U-turn, and then headed down the driveway. He flashed her a sexy grin, a grin filled with the promise of forbidden sexual delights. Desire rushed Star, flooded her, and she couldn't stand not knowing another second. She wanted an end to her virginity now.

"Pull over."

"What?" He glanced at her, and he must have seen the desire on her face because he practically skidded off the road. He threw the truck into park, cut the engine, and reached for Star, dragging her across his lap.

And Star knew. The wait was finally over.

CHAPTER THIRTEEN

Star couldn't get her clothes off fast enough.

Cade helped, lifting the hem of her T-shirt up and over her head.

"Beautiful," he murmured when he caught sight of her lacy white bra, his hands bracketing her waist.

Star sat on his lap, facing him, the steering wheel at her back, yet she wasn't uncomfortable; she was way past that. It were as if a fever had overtaken her body; hot all over, she burned from the inside out.

Cade separated from her slightly and shucked his own shirt. The minute he was free, he drew her to him, kissing her, scattering what was left of her inhibitions.

Her bra disappeared. Her shorts were magically unzipped.

She unbuttoned Cade's jeans and he lifted his butt to free his sex.

Star couldn't look away. She'd seen men naked in pictures, but never like this, nothing like this. Unable to help herself, she touched him.

He jerked as if she'd scorched his skin.

"Sorry," he rasped. "Feels too good."

Star had no idea why he'd be sorry about that. She smiled. Cade helped her get her shorts off, and for a second she caught the mental image of how funny they must look, twisted together as they fought the shorts and her panties.

Before she could right herself, Cade lifted her, setting her back on his lap so she straddled him, facing him. He kissed her lips, her neck, her breasts, the sensations exquisite.

And Star kissed him back. Devoured him. Let him touch her any way he wanted to.

"You brought protection, right?" Star asked.

"Of course." He shifted her again and removed a condom from the front pocket of his jeans. Star watched, fascinated, as he rolled the protection on. Suited up, he settled Star back in his lap.

She expected pain the first time, but prayed she wouldn't have any. Surely the barrier of her virginity was long gone. Briefly, she wondered if he'd be able to tell she was a virgin, but as quickly as she had the thought, she discarded it. She didn't care.

Star braced her hands on Cade's shoulders. Waited as he tried to enter her, and when he did, she couldn't stop the small gasp that came from her throat. She tensed, her nails digging into his shoulders.

Cade stilled. He knew.

"Star?" he said.

"Don't stop now," Star said. "The worst is over."

"You're a virgin?" he asked, his eyes filled with questions. "How is that possible?"

"The usual way." Again, Star wished for darkness. "Do we have to have this conversation now?"

"Yes." He'd quit moving, but was still inside her, every bit as aroused as he'd been moments before.

"Oh, come on." She shifted a little, testing for pain, but found none.

"Stop it, Star."

"No." She moved some more. "I've waited a long time for

this, and you're ruining it for me, O'Brien." She shifted again, then leaned forward and whispered in his ear, "Show me what I've been missing. Make it worth the wait." She kissed his neck, letting her tongue linger against his skin.

His fingers tightened on her hips and Star knew she had him back.

From that point forward, things moved so fast Star could barely hold on. She struggled to keep up, to match Cade's rhythm, then suddenly, he stilled. Was that it? There had to be more, didn't there?

"Sorry," he said, the word rough and filled with need. "I tried to hold back, to wait, but you feel too good."

"What do you mean?" she asked, not sure she understood.

"You didn't finish."

"I didn't?"

He glanced away from her, then back. "You'd know if you had, Star."

All her doubts, all her insecurities assaulted her. She'd done something wrong. Maybe she *was* broken inside. Good grief, could she be the one woman in her family that wasn't good at sex? And worse, she was pretty sure she had the imprint of the steering wheel on her back.

He smoothed the hair from her forehead. "What are you thinking, Star?"

"That I have no idea what I'm doing," she said, sounding completely forlorn.

He smiled. "I can teach you, but not here in the truck. You caught me off guard. I'm sorry your first time wasn't everything it should have been." His hands moved up and down her back, soothing.

"You mean I'm not broken?" A measure of relief filled her.

"Baby, far from it." He grinned. "Why didn't you tell me?"

"I didn't think it was important."

"It was important to me," Cade said. "Star, we're in a truck. Your first time should have been somewhere special."

"It's not about the place," Star said. "It's about the person.

I don't care where we are."

He sighed. "At least we used a condom."

"I'm not that stupid," she said. "I'm not about to get pregnant. I brought my own condom just in case this happened. Plus, I'm pretty sure it's not the time of month when I can get pregnant."

"I hope you're right." Cade lifted her from him and set her back in the passenger seat. "The last thing we need around here is another pregnancy."

"I agree." Star started to shake. Pregnancy wasn't an option. Yet, she'd let the moment sweep her away without giving much thought to protection. What if something had gone wrong? How dumb was she? Star searched for her underwear. She shimmed into her panties, put on her bra. Cade passed her T-shirt to her.

The silence in the truck grew thick as they dressed.

Cade reached into the back seat and handed her a jacket. "Put this on."

"I don't know why I'm shaking. It's warm out."

"Trauma."

"There's been no trauma here," she assured him. "I'm a big girl. I'm fine."

"Are you, Star?"

She leveled a look at him. Her spine stiffened. "I'm fine. People have sex all the time. I'm a big girl. I can handle it."

"Next time will be better," Cade said with conviction. "I promise."

Star nodded. She wanted a next time, wanted to have as many next times as she could before she left him behind.

She really was a Cosmo girl after all.

* * *

Cade let himself into the house and crept up the stairs. He went into his bedroom and closed the door.

Holy crap.

He plopped down on the edge of the bed, his head in his hands. Star. A virgin. Who would have guessed? Not him, that's for sure. She always seemed so arrogant, so in control, so big city. He figured she'd be the same way in bed.

What now? Should he marry her? Cade fell back onto the bed. Where had that stupid thought come from? They weren't living in the 1800s for cripe's sake. Any marriage between them would be sure to end in disaster. She would never stay here in Seward, and he wasn't about to leave. Was he habitually attracted to city girls? What the heck was his problem? Plus, she didn't want kids. Great.

Wait, they weren't talking about marriage. This was about sex. He'd let her take the lead. More than anything, he needed another shot with her. He needed to make love to Star again.

And this time, he'd make sure that she knew she'd finished.

* * *

"I should probably go," Star said, passing baby Will back to Brandi. They'd just spent an hour visiting, with Star filling Brandi in on Destiny's exploits. She didn't, however, tell Brandi anything about the night she'd spent with Cade. She couldn't bring herself to talk about something so private and personal. "I have to stop by Evan's."

"He's sweet on you, you know." Brandi took Will from Star, cradling the baby against her chest. "Evan Jenson wants you, Star."

"He's a flirt, for sure. But I'm not the one he wants. I think he's hot for Vivienne."

"Vivienne? You're way prettier than the French pop tart." Brandi moved Will to her other shoulder. "Talk around town is Evan's great in bed."

"Yuck. I'm not that kind of girl."

Brandi laughed. "No, you're definitely not that kind of girl. Any forward progress with Cade?"

"No," Star lied.

"I still think you should give Cade a chance."

If Brandi only knew. "I'm fine with things the way they are."

Brandi gave her a skeptical look. "Call me if you need

125

anything, sis."

"I will."

Star leaned down and kissed Will's soft cheek. "Bye, baby." Then she kissed Brandi. "See you later."

Star left Brandi's and drove the six miles to Evan Jenson's cabin. She had some samples to drop off, and she wanted to take a couple more still shots for Vivienne. The designer had sent her a list, via email, of questions about Evan. Did he have a girlfriend? What was he like in person? What could Star tell her about him? Star wondered about the questions, but she'd emailed back her answers. Something was definitely up between Evan and Vivienne. Maybe Evan had made his love connection before the show even aired. A match between Evan and Vivienne would boost ratings considerably. Frank would love it.

Evan met her in the driveway, and Star had to admit Brandi was right. He was a handsome man: big, tall, and all muscle. But he wasn't Cade. Cade had wormed his way into her life a long time ago. She knew the worst parts of him, and oddly enough, she trusted him now.

Evan met her at her car, opening her door.

"Hey, pretty lady." His velvet eyes twinkled. No wonder women loved him.

Star got out of the car. "I've got those samples."

"Great."

Star unloaded the book of swatches Vivienne had sent. "I'll bring these in if you get the tile and granite samples."

"Sure thing," Evan said as he easily lifted the samples from the trunk.

When they were inside, Star spread everything out on the counter. "Look through all of this. Vivienne will be in touch."

"Oh, we're in touch." Evan grinned, the kind of grin you get when you have a delicious secret.

Star's antenna went up. "Exactly what is going on between the two of you?"

"A little long distance flirting," Evan admitted.

Evan flirted with everyone. Vivienne flirted with everyone.

A match made in heaven, or in hell? Who knew? Hormones were hormones. She couldn't control what happened between Evan and Vivienne any more than she could control what happened between Cade and herself.

"Coffee?" Evan asked when she caught him staring at her.

"I should get going," Star said. "I've been gone all day and my mother is in the middle of a meltdown."

He laughed. "One cup of coffee? Come on, Star. I'm a lonely guy. Take pity on me."

He really was a nice guy, and so far he'd been a good sport when it came to Vivienne's ideas. Star caved. "Okay."

They took their coffee out on the deck, and Star was again struck by the beauty of the place. His plane rested next to dock, like a bright white bird against the startling blue of the water.

"You know," she said. "You should get prepared for the offers of marriage you're going to get once the piece airs. You've got a little slice of heaven here."

He spread his arms wide. "Bring them on. They are part of my master plan."

"Your master plan?" she asked, not understanding.

"How else am I going to make the lovely Vivienne jealous?"

"Jealous?" Star sipped her coffee.

"She has a wild side," Evan said. "And I like 'em wild. You know what they say, there's someone out there for everyone."

"I wonder," Star said.

"There's a guy out there for you, Star."

"I don't know about that." She smiled wistfully. "I'm more into my career."

"Really?" Evan squinted at her. "I don't see it. You're an Alaska girl. A hometown star. You fit here."

She laughed. "This is the last place I'd fit."

He shook his head. "Nope. You belong here, in the wild, in this town."

As Star drove home from Evan's she couldn't shake his words. She didn't fit here. She didn't want to fit here. She hated Alaska.

More than ever, she couldn't wait to get home to her brand new condo, to all the smooth granite and the scent of freshly laid hardwood floors. Once she was there all this silly doubt would go away.

She was sure of it.

CHAPTER FOURTEEN

The following day, Star finished up at Evan Jenson's, seeing to the last minute details. Evan seemed good with everything Vivienne suggested. He loved the deep greens and beiges of the color scheme. He loved how the designer had managed to bring the outdoors in, layering different textures, selecting an eclectic assortment of textiles.

Star left Evan's place satisfied that the filming of his home restoration would go smoothly. She was free to leave Alaska now. Her part of the show was done. A week from Monday the crew would come up, ready to roll, and she'd be home, enjoying her new condo.

Star waited for the feeling of satisfaction to come, but oddly, her emotions were mixed. A part of her hated to leave Brandi, and another part of her wasn't done with Cade yet. As much as she wanted to, she couldn't just walk away from him. Cade stirred something inside her, brought to life a spark that she wanted to fan into a flame, an inferno of, well, lust. Was this desire, the one sensation that had always managed to elude her?

The thought troubled Star as she cruised down the highway, the road a wide open runway. There wasn't another car in sight. At home, negotiating I-5 took a master's in defensive driving. As she drove she marveled at the slow,

JOLEEN JAMES

almost comatose pace of life here. Alaska had been fun for a while, but she needed the stimulation of the city, needed the energy, she even needed the traffic.

Star didn't bother with her turn signal and pulled into Patsy's driveway. Right away, she spotted the note pinned to the front door. Star turned off the ignition, left the car, and removed the note.

Trudy's in labor. Where are you, Destiny? I have guests coming and I need you. Cade

Trudy was in labor? Where was her mother?

Afraid she knew the answer to Cade's question; Star let herself into the mobile home and walked straight to the bedroom. The bed had been stripped, the sheets in a wad on the floor. Destiny's hot pink suitcases were gone. Back in the kitchen, Star found another note. Quickly, she scanned the paper. Her mother was gone, to Canada, with John. Gone. Without so much as a goodbye.

Star wondered if her mother had even bothered to say goodbye to Brandi. Disappointment filled Star's chest, the pain almost unbearable, yet all too familiar. Why was her mother such a coward? Once again Destiny had left Star to pick up the pieces. Obviously, her mother hadn't bothered to quit her job with the O'Briens.

With a heavy heart, Star headed for Cade's. A part of her didn't want to clean up her mother's mess, but the more responsible side of her said she had to pitch in, help fill the void her mother's departure had left behind.

Two minutes later Star pulled into Cade's driveway. She exited the car and walked quickly to the door, knocked once, and let herself in.

Brad came out of the kitchen, Emma behind him.

"How's Trudy?" Star asked.

Emma, seeing Star, broke free, running straight for her. She flung her little arms around Star's legs.

"Water came out of Trudy." Emma tilted her head back to look at Star, her eyes wide. "She's hurt."

"Hurt?" Star looked to Brad for confirmation while

stroking the top of Emma's head.

"She's in labor," Brad confirmed, suddenly looking more mature than his sixteen years. "Uncle Ron took her to the hospital."

"Where's your dad?"

"In the kitchen," Brad said.

Star started forward, pausing to unwrap Emma from her legs. Star squatted in front of the little girl. "Sweetie, it's okay. Water was supposed to come out of Trudy. It just means the baby is ready to be born."

"Really?" Emma asked with a sniff.

"Really," Star confirmed with a smile. She stood and held her hand out to Emma. "Now come on, let's go and find your dad."

Together, Brad, Emma, and Star went into the kitchen. Cade stood at the counter, chopping carrots.

"Hey," she said.

He glanced up, the wrinkles in his forehead easing into relief. "Star. You heard about Trudy?"

"Yes, what can I do to help?"

Brad and Emma each took a barstool at the counter.

"Find your mother and get her here," Cade said, slapping Brad's hand away as he snagged a carrot slice. "She's not answering her phone. I've got a plane to meet. I need her here."

"No can do," Star said. "She's gone. She left for Anchorage. She's going with John to Canada."

"What?" Cade set the knife down with a thud. "I guess I'm not surprised."

"I'm sorry," Star offered.

"Are you okay?" Cade's tender tone was nearly her undoing. She hadn't expected his compassion. In fact, she'd expected the opposite, anger.

His soft inquiry brought both Emma and Brad's eyes to her.

Suddenly uncomfortable, Star said, "I'll be fine. I'm used to my mother letting me down. You're not. Look, let me go and pick up the guests."

Cade walked to her, took her hand, his fingers warm and strong. "That would be great, Star."

"I'll help out tonight," she said, wanting to make things right.

"Are you sure?" Cade asked. "You don't have to fill in for Destiny. It's not your fault she's irresponsible."

"I know that," Star said. "I wish I understood her better, you know? How can she walk away, without any thought to the consequences? What kind of person does that?"

"I don't know," Cade replied with a sad shake of his head.

"I don't know why I feel so betrayed," Star said. "It's not like this is the first time she's abandoned me. I feel so bad for Brandi. She's going to take the news of Mom's departure hard."

"I'm sorry," Cade said, squeezing her fingers. "More than you know. I wish I could take away your pain."

His sweet words brought a smile to Star's lips. "What time is the plane due?"

"Now. Seward airport. I was about to take off."

"How many guests?" she asked, the business side of herself taking over.

"Two. Brad," Cade said. "Get the itinerary for Star. All the info's on it, flight number, guest names, etc."

"Okay." Brad slid from the bar stool and left the room.

"Can I ride along, Star?" Emma asked. "I can make you feel better."

The little girl's concern touched Star's heart. "That's sweet, Em," Star said.

"No," Cade cut in. "I need you to go out back and find Finn. You can make Star feel better later."

"Aw, okay." Emma stuck her lower lip out. Her feet dragged on her way to the back door.

Brad returned with the itinerary. Star took it from him, noting the guests' names, Hank Crawford and Jack Taylor. She glanced at the flight plan. The men were from Texas.

"Okay," Star said. "I'm on my way."

"Take the van." Cade removed the keys from a hook near the back door and tossed them to her.

Star caught the keys.

"Thanks, Star," Cade said, his tone warm.

"No problem."

Star backed the van out of the driveway. When she reached the airport, the plane was there. She was so busy looking for Cade's guests that she was caught totally unaware when a woman said, "How did you know I was coming?"

Star whirled around at the familiar French accent.

Vivienne stood on the tarmac, her smile wide.

* * *

For a small town, Seward was proving to be a hotbed of activity. Star never expected to find Vivienne at the airport and she had a million questions for the designer, all of which had to wait. Vivienne, needing to freshen up, had gone up to her room—a room she was lucky Cade had available, along with Cade's other guests.

At loose ends, Cade had suggested Star go out back and relax in the hammock while he finished getting dinner ready. Thinking some time in the hammock sounded wonderful, she'd headed outside.

Star rolled into the hammock, her eyes on the sky. White, fluffy clouds drifted by.

"What'cha doin'?" Finn asked.

The twins walked up, looking a little worse for wear. Finn's white shirt had a red stain on it, and his knees were filthy. Emma's pigtails had unraveled, and her face held the remains of what Star hoped was chocolate ice cream.

"I'm daydreaming," Star said.

"What's that?" Emma asked, rubbing her eyes.

"It means I'm letting my mind wander where it wants to go. It's a time to think about nothing or to think about your wildest dreams."

"Can we play?" Emma asked.

"Sure, I guess," Star said.

Emma started to climb in the hammock. Star held on, making room for the little girl. Finn went around to the other side and got in, too.

For a few seconds the hammock swung madly, but then it settled down to a slight sway.

Emma snuggled against Star, throwing her little arm across Star's stomach. Finn, all boy, stayed on his back, his eyes trained on the sky.

"This feels good," Star said. The hammock rocked beneath them. "A little down time is good."

"What's down time?" Emma asked, her eyes on Star.

"You know," Star said. "Time to relax."

"Are you still sad about your mother, Star?" Emma asked. "I still get sad about my mother sometimes."

"Of course you do." Star took Emma's hand, knowing the little girl's ache for her mother was a million times worse than her own.

Emma's fingers tightened around Star's. "What are you going to dream about, Star?"

"I don't know," Star said, but Cade popped into her head. She didn't allow herself to daydream about him. What good would it do? Sex. Yes, she'd definitely daydream about sex with Cade, if the kids weren't here. No, for now her daydreams needed to be G-rated. "I'm dreaming about my new condo."

Finn shifted beside her. "What's a condo?"

"It's like a house. It's where I live. I just moved in and I haven't been home to enjoy it in a long time."

"I don't want you to go, Star," Emma said resolutely.

"Thanks, sweetie," Star said, rubbing the little girl's arm. "But it's time for me to go home."

"Will you come back to visit?" Emma asked.

"Of course. Brandi, Bud, and Will are here." Thinking about leaving brought a funny ache to Star's chest. "You guys are here."

Emma nodded, happy with Star's answer.

"What will you daydream about, Em?" Star asked.

"Ponies, and Snowbell, and chocolate milk."

Star grinned. "Wow. How about you, Finn?"

"My bird trap," Finn said. "I built it today."

"And I helped," Emma chimed in.

"Did you catch one?" Star asked.

"Not yet." Finn looked at her. "But I will. I put some breadcrumbs in the trap. If a bird goes inside, the box will fall and trap it."

"What will you do with the bird if you catch it?" Star asked.

"It will be our pet," Emma said, her eyes all dreamy.

Star prayed they wouldn't catch anything. She didn't have the heart to tell the twins that wild birds didn't make good pets.

Finn leaned more fully against her right side; Emma cuddled against her left side, their little bodies soft and heavy. Star closed her eyes and relaxed. She could hear the sound of silverware clinking together as Cade got things ready for the evening meal. The high whine of a hairdryer came from the upstairs bathroom window. Probably Vivienne.

Exhaustion claimed Star and it suddenly felt like she hadn't slept in days. Emma burrowed more securely against her. Star's fingers smoothed the little girl's hair. On her other side, she could feel the rise and fall of Finn's chest.

Star drifted off. The slap of the screen door woke her, followed by Brad saying, "Dad, the stove timer's going off."

Star opened her eyes to find Cade watching her. How long had he been standing there beside the hammock? Instantly self-conscious, Star tried to sit up, but the kids held her in place.

"Don't move," Cade said softly. "I want to remember you like this."

Star didn't want him to remember her like this, like she was a mother. This wasn't her at all, and this wasn't the image she wanted him to have of her. She moved again, and woke Emma. The little girl sat up, nearly dumping them all out of the hammock.

"Hey," Finn cried, grabbing onto a handful of Star's shirt to keep from falling.

The blissful moment with the kids shattered. Cade lifted Emma out of the hammock. Finn jumped out, and then Cade reached for Star, pulling her up.

"Go wash up for dinner," Cade said to the kids, his hands still on Star's arms. "Hands and faces. Change your shirts, and comb your hair."

"Aw, heck," Finn grumbled on the way to his house, Emma right behind him.

"I fell asleep," Star said. "I guess the past couple of nights are catching up with me."

"You look good with my kids, Star," Cade said his hands still on her arms. "They really like you."

"I like them, too," Star said. "I never said I didn't like kids. I just don't want any of my own."

Cade's hands slid down her arms, and he took her hands in his. "Okay. I respect that. I didn't mean anything by it. I'll take you any way I can get you, Star White."

"I like the sound of that."

"Mmmm," he murmured, his fingers playing against hers. "I'm glad."

Star smiled up at him.

"Thanks for helping out tonight." He let go of one of her hands, and still holding the other one, they started toward the house. "I owe you, and I think I know just how to repay you."

His words held a sexy, seductive edge.

Star's stomach rippled with desire. "Is that so?"

"Count on it."

The promise and heat in his stare almost made Star forget they had to get through the evening meal before they could be alone. Her nerve endings crackled, as if they'd been electrically charged—just looking at Cade sent pleasure through her clear to her toes.

More than ever she wanted one more night with Cade, one more chance to see if she really was capable of letting go and enjoying sex. One more chance with Cade before she left him and Alaska behind.

CHAPTER FIFTEEN

"This house is begging for *Update This!*" Vivienne said as she scanned the O'Brien kitchen.

"I know," Star agreed as she put away the last of the silverware. Dinner had taken forever. She'd been unable to eat after her encounter with Cade, her stomach too tight in anticipation of the evening yet to come.

Star and Vivienne stood together in Cade's kitchen, and Star looked at the room with a designer's eyes. The linoleum was worn, the counter tops dated, the sink stained and well used. "Too bad we don't have time for one more room." She smiled. "Not that Cade would let us do it. He likes the place the way it is. He's not big into change."

"Maybe he could be persuaded, yes?" Vivienne asked with a cat-like smile. "I saw the way he was looking at you at dinner. *Ooh la la.*"

Star shook her head. "Why are you here so early anyway?" She folded the dishtowel and hung it on the bar near the sink.

"I promised Evan I would fly in for a final sit down before we begin taping. He had some concerns I want to address in person."

"He didn't mention any concerns to me," Star said. "He seemed to love everything you've suggested, even that wicked saw blade above the bed."

"Oh, that. Nothing like a little danger in the bedroom."
She laughed. "Seriously, we've been talking via email and
telephone. Anyway, I'm here now. He's expecting me in the
morning."

"I'll take you over."

Vivienne waved her hand. "No, no. He's picking me up at
nine a.m. sharp."

Star's eyes narrowed on the designer. "What's really going
on?"

"Nothing," Vivienne said too quickly. "I told you. He has
concerns. Frank wants me to hold his hand."

"That's my job," Star said. "And I've done it. Give it up."

"Oh, all right." Vivienne sighed. "Evan invited me up
early. We've developed a long distance relationship. You've
seen him, Star. He is magnificent. He invited me to see the
sights."

"And Frank's okay with this?" Star asked, still skeptical.

"I didn't exactly tell him," Vivienne said. "We wrapped up
the shoot in Fairbanks and I took a detour here."

"I see."

"Don't be mad." Vivienne pursed her full lips. "I know
what I'm doing, Star."

Star shrugged. "Okay."

Cade and the Texans came into the kitchen, halting their
conversation.

"We're going to call it a night," Hank said. "Five a.m.
comes early."

Jack tipped his head. "Thanks for everything, Cade. Good
night, ladies."

"Good night," Star said.

"*Bonne nuit!* Hank, Jack." Vivienne blew them a kiss.

"*Bonne nuit!*" the men echoed, their Texas twangs totally
obliterating the beautiful French words for good night. The
men headed upstairs.

"I'm going to bed, too." Vivienne yawned. "Thank you for
a wonderful meal." She kissed Star's cheek. "Don't worry
about me. I'll be fine."

"I hope so," Star said.

"Good night, Vivienne," Cade said.

Vivienne waved. "See you in the morning, you two. Don't do anything I wouldn't do."

"Alone at last," Cade said when the designer was gone. He reached for Star.

Star stepped into his arms as if it were the most natural thing in the world, her hands sliding up his toned back. "You feel good, O'Brien."

He grinned. "Baby, you haven't felt anything yet."

Star laughed. Cade's lips brushed against hers. Her heart sped up. She wanted this, wanted him.

The phone rang, the bell cutting the sexual tension between them.

"It might be Ron." Cade reached around Star, and picked up the call. "Hello?" He smiled. "Congratulations, Ron. A boy. That's great news. Is Trudy okay?" Cade listened, a smile on his face. "Well, get some rest. Yes, Finn's fine, everyone's fine. The guests just went up for the night." A pause. "No, don't worry about tomorrow, I've got it covered. Star's offered to stay here with the kids." Cade's eyes caressed her. "Yeah, she's great and the kids love her."

Again with the kids. Star really did hope he wasn't getting the wrong idea.

"Okay. Good night." Cade hung up the phone.

"A boy," Star said.

"Six pounds, six ounces."

"Wow."

"Are you sure you're okay with helping out tomorrow?" Cade asked. "The kids can really be a handful."

"I'm a great babysitter," Star said. "Believe me; I've had years of experience."

"You only have four nights left here," Cade said, as if she weren't fully aware.

"I know."

His arms circled her again. "Spend them with me, Star."

She wanted to. Big time. "How? The kids are here."

"I know." He touched his forehead to hers. "At least stay with me, keep me company. I'll figure out a way for us to be alone."

Star lifted her mouth to his, kissing him. Cade deepened the kiss. About to lose herself completely to him, to the hard feel of his body against hers, to the erotic warmth of his mouth, she broke the kiss, fighting to get her bearings.

"Where's Brad?" she asked.

"He left after dinner. Went to town to see a movie with Tyler and his parents."

"What happened to the grounding?"

Cade smiled. "I was hoping to get lucky. Sue me. I'm a bad parent." He kissed her again.

"And the twins?" she asked.

"Are asleep." He kissed her forehead, her cheek, her neck. Her thoughts scattered. Desire beat a wild rhythm through her veins. She didn't want to stop him. She drowned in sensation, her limbs turning to mush.

They kissed their way to the family room, to the couch. Together, they sank into the softness. Cade's hands roamed freely under her T-shirt, as if he were trying to memorize every inch of her. Her bra unhooked. His hands closed over her breasts. Star's nipples hardened as they pressed into his palms. His fingers found the button on her shorts.

"Cade," she rasped. "We shouldn't. Not here."

"I just want to touch you. I'll keep your clothes on."

It were as if they were teenagers, sneaking around, afraid to be caught. "The kids," Star reminded him.

"Are asleep."

"The guests," she said faintly.

Cade left her and closed the door on the family room, twisting the lock. "Okay?"

"Okay," she said, making room for him on the couch.

His hand slipped under the waistband of her shorts, inside the lace of her panties. He cupped her, and Star couldn't help it, a soft moan left her lips. Before she could feel embarrassed, his fingers moved lower, touching her, stroking her, the sensation unlike anything she'd ever felt before.

His mouth drifted to her neck, kissed the hollow at the base of her throat. Star let her leg fall to the side, giving him greater access, and he took it. He played her like an expert, and then it happened...something inside of Star shifted. She went weightless, a spiral of lust vibrated through her, took her away, left her gasping.

Stunned by the sensation, she couldn't speak or move. Her entire body came alive in a way she couldn't put to words.

Cade shifted, moving so he was full on top of her. She could feel his erection through her shorts as he pressed against her sensitive area.

"Cade, did I—" She broke off, embarrassed.

"Yes," he whispered against her mouth. "Now I want my turn."

"But," she protested weakly.

"Quit worrying."

He pulled her clothes off, and Star let him. She was way past the stopping point. She didn't care anymore, didn't care if Brad walked in or the kids woke, she just wanted him inside her.

Quickly, Cade rolled on a condom.

And it was different this time. She arched, ready for him.

"Show me what to do," she said, wanting to please him.

"Meet me." He demonstrated, using his hands to guide her.

Star caught on quickly. Her fingers dug into his back and she held on. She focused on a myriad of sensations. This time, she knew what to expect and she let the friction lure her back into an orgasm, and when it happened, Cade came with her, moaning deep in his throat.

She became every cliché she'd ever read about. She floated on air. The earth moved. Her skin tingled. Clichés, all, but she experienced every one of them.

"Uh, oh," Cade said.

"What?" Star asked, not wanting to talk or move. She just wanted to be.

"The condom," he said. "It broke."

"What?" Star stared at him, sure she'd heard him wrong. "What do you mean it broke?"

Cade shifted, showing her the torn condom. "Don't worry. You said you didn't think you could get pregnant this time of the month, right?"

They separated. Star glanced around, looking for her clothes. "Right. No. I don't know. What should I do? I can't get pregnant."

"Shower?" Cade suggested.

"I need to go." Star began to dress. Her stomach churned. This was her fault. She should have used double birth control, triple. What was she thinking?

"Hey," Cade said, touching her arm. "It's okay. No matter what, it'll be okay."

Star looked at him as if he were crazy. "It's not okay," she said on her way to the door. "You don't understand. I can't be pregnant."

"Don't go."

"I have to." Star ran from the room.

"Star," Cade called.

Star didn't stop, she just kept running.

* * *

Cade yanked his clothes on, all the while unable to believe his bad luck. A broken condom. Man. And there'd been no mistaking the panic on Star's face. She really did not want kids. Period.

Dressed, Cade took off after Star, finding her on the porch.

When she saw him, she said, "Go away. Please." Her eyes had a glassy look, as if she'd been crying.

Cade ignored her and sat down beside her. "You're overreacting. I'm sure everything's fine. It was a small tear."

"I can't be pregnant." She shook her head, then looked at him. "I don't want children, Cade. Ever."

He took her words like a kick to the gut.

"I had a terrible childhood," she said sadly. "My mother's been married five times. I've lived with four stepfathers, including one who thought he'd take a try at me."

"What?" Cade said, struggling to grasp all she told him. "Star."

"Don't worry," she said quickly. "Obviously, he didn't get anywhere. My mother happened to come home. She divorced him, pronto."

Relief filled Cade. "Thank God."

"I raised my sisters," Star said. "When we lived with my mom, I was the mother. I know how it feels when a child gets hurt or sick. I know that responsibility." She put her hand over her heart. "You got a look firsthand look at my mother today. She's a train wreck. She left all the time when we were small. Then we'd wind up with Patsy."

"Okay," Cade said. "But you were a child yourself. You're a woman now. You're better equipped to deal with a child."

"I'm not," she said sadly. "I'm emotionally stunted. Used up. I don't want a child. I don't want to be responsible for anyone's children, even yours."

"You're selling yourself short," Cade said. "You did a great job with your sisters."

She laughed, the sound manic. "I did not. Ruby Sue got pregnant when she was fifteen, remember? And Tawney is a dancer in a topless show. Where's her self-esteem? It's in the toilet."

"Come on," Cade said. "You did the best you could. The real blame needs to go to your mother."

"Maybe."

"So when you were here, in Seward, what was that like for you?" Cade asked, wanting to understand her.

She smiled softly. "Wonderful. Patsy took care of all of us, including me. I didn't have to be the mother." Her eyes filled with tears. "I loved her so much. I used to wish she was my mother."

Cade's stomach flipped as the full weight of his actions toward Star hit him. "I'm sorry. I didn't get it, any of it. I must have been your worst nightmare when you were a kid." He'd bullied a little girl who'd already taken so many hard knocks. It was like he'd kicked a puppy, or worse.

She looked at him. "So you understand why I'm so freaked out? I don't want to be a mother. It's just not in the cards for me."

"And if you are pregnant?" Cade asked, afraid to hear the answer.

"I can't think about that." Star rose. "It's late. I'm going home."

"Star."

"Go inside to your kids, O'Brien."

She walked away, leaving him to stare after her, an ache in his heart.

* * *

Star's alarm jolted her awake. Four-thirty a.m. The events of last night came flooding back. She'd made love with Cade. Wonderful, mind-blowing sex. The condom had broken. The soul-baring conversation on her porch.

Star groaned.

She turned over on Patsy's couch, noting the soreness between her thighs. What had started out as a perfect night had turned into a nightmare. She prayed for the millionth time the condom had protected her.

Star hugged the pillow to her chest. She knew she needed to get up and get over to Cade's. She'd promised to be there right before five a.m. to stay with kids while he fished, but the thought of facing him kept her where she was.

Star glanced at the clock. She had to get up, now. She rolled out of bed and into the shower. The hot water helped wake her up. She dressed quickly in a jean skirt and white sleeveless blouse, sliding her feet into the blue flip flops.

The sky was pink as she drove to Cade's. Star pulled into the driveway and cut the engine. How would Cade greet her this morning? For a second, nerves tightened her stomach. Stop it, Star, she told herself. You have nothing to be nervous

JOLEEN JAMES

about. You're both adults.

More confident, she strode to the house and let herself in. The scents of bacon and coffee filled the air. She could hear the men talking in the kitchen.

Yet, she couldn't stop the blush that heated her cheeks when she entered the kitchen. "Hey, everyone."

"Mornin', Star," Hank and Jack said at the same time. Both men worked to eat the food on their plates.

Her attention moved onto Cade.

"Good morning," he said warmly, looking her straight in the eye. He smiled. "You okay this morning?"

"Sure," she lied.

"Breakfast?" he asked, but she didn't miss the worry crease on his brow.

"Looks good, but I think I'll start with coffee. It's a little early for food."

"Help yourself." He gave a head nod toward the pot.

"Thanks." Star snagged a coffee cup.

Brad wandered into the kitchen, looking rumpled and exhausted.

Cade set a plate of food in front of him. "Eat, we take off in fifteen minutes."

"I'm not hungry," Brad grumbled.

"You will be once we're on the boat," Cade said as he took his place at the table.

Hank and Jack filled the conversation with their excitement over the upcoming trip. Cade chimed in, and even Brad had something to say about netting a halibut.

To her surprise, Star enjoyed the men's banter. She sipped her coffee, glad for the safe subjects. She didn't want to think about a possible pregnancy.

More than ever, she wanted to go home. Alaska was a dead end. No career. Nothing but fish. And one hot man.

No, Cade wasn't a fair trade off for a life filled with fish, kids, and second-rate furnishings.

"Star's a lifesaver," Cade said, to the men, "giving up her free time to be here to help."

146

His eyes said all the things he couldn't—he liked having her here. Ignoring the bittersweet ache in her chest, Star said, "My pleasure. I've enjoyed being here, meeting the kids, seeing the place with adult eyes."

They finished eating, and Brad took the men out to the van.

"Thanks again, Star," Cade said on his way out. "The twins will be up soon."

"We'll be fine," Star assured him.

He touched her chin, lifting it slightly. "I'll see you later." His lips brushed against hers. "I can tell you're worried. Relax. We'll talk when I get home."

"Okay," she whispered against his lips. "Don't worry about things here. As soon as Vivienne leaves I'm going to take the kids to see their new cousin."

"They'll love that," Cade said.

"Come on, Dad," Brad called from the foyer.

Cade kissed her quick. "Bye."

Star was left to stare after him. The broken condom aside, she was going to miss Cade when she left.

She was going to miss him a lot.

CHAPTER SIXTEEN

"He's so beautiful." From her perch on the side of Trudy's hospital bed, Star leaned in to touch the soft hair on the baby's head. Safe in the circle of Trudy's arms, he moved, emitting a small squeak that brought a smile to Star's lips. "What're you going to name him?"

"Daniel," Trudy said in a dreamy voice. "After Ron's dad."

Star smiled. She glanced at Finn and Emma who had climbed up onto the foot of the bed. "What do you guys think of your new cousin?"

Finn frowned. "He's wrinkly."

"He's so cute," Emma said, reaching over to touch the top of Daniel's head. "Can I hold him, Trudy?"

"Sure, honey," Trudy said. "Sit over there in the easy chair. Star, can you help her?"

"Of course." Star settled Emma in the oversized chair, putting a pillow next to the little girl for support. Star took baby Daniel from Trudy's arms. Daniel yawned, his mouth making a round little o.

"This sure has been my summer for babies," Star said as she placed the baby in Emma's arms. Again, she gave a silent prayer that she wouldn't be joining the baby club.

Daniel squeaked again, sounding more like a kitten than a human baby. Star scooted in next to Emma, placing her arm around the little girl, her hand near Daniel, in case Emma needed help.

"You look different today, Star," Trudy said, giving Star a measuring glance.

"How so?" Star asked.

"I'm not sure. You look softer somehow."

"Well, I have been on vacation, sort of." Star smiled.

"Hmmm." Trudy pursed her lips, as if she were trying to figure Star out.

"Where's Finn?" Star asked, realizing the little boy was no longer in the room.

Trudy glanced around. "I don't know. He was here a minute ago. Maybe he took off after Ron and headed down to the cafeteria."

"Here, Em," Star said. "Let me give Daniel back to Trudy for a minute. I've got to go and get Finn."

Emma offered Star the baby and she moved him to his mother's waiting arms. "Stay here," she said to Emma.

In the hall, Star called, "Finn?"

She didn't see the boy anywhere. She remembered a candy machine near the elevators. Maybe he'd gone there. At the machine, no Finn. Panic fluttered in her chest. A woman in lavender scrubs passed by.

"Excuse me," Star said, no mistaking the urgency in her tone. "I'm looking for a little boy. He has black hair and blue eyes."

"I haven't seen him," the woman said. "Sorry."

Star went back the way she'd come. At the nurses' station, she gave the woman there Finn's description, but the woman had no memory of Finn.

Star's heart banged in her chest as she took the elevator to the floor where the cafeteria was. In the cafeteria, she quickly located Ron.

"Where's Finn?" she asked.

Ron snapped the lid onto his coffee. "He was with you last time I saw him. Why?"

"I can't find him." Her heart racing, Star whirled away,

running for the front desk.

"Did you see a little boy come by here?" she asked the receptionist.

"Sweetie, I've seen a lot of people," the woman replied. "This is a busy place."

Ron joined her. "What's going on?"

"I can't find Finn," Star said, panic thick in her chest. "I lost him. I can't believe I lost him."

"Get a grip." Ron took her arm. "He's here somewhere."

"He wouldn't leave the hospital, would he?" Star asked.

"Let's check the car, just to be sure." Ron propelled her to the doors. Together they exited the hospital.

Star ran out to the parking lot, looking around wildly. Ron came to a stop beside her.

And then she saw him—them. Finn and Cade. They came around the side of Cade's truck toward her.

Relief hit Star, nearly bringing her to her knees. She paused, her hand going to her heart. "Finn," she cried, unable to keep the panic from her tone, "I've been looking for you."

Cade glanced down at Finn. "You came out here without telling anyone?"

Finn shrugged. "I saw you out the window. They were busy with the baby."

"Star," Cade said, his expression contrite. "I'm sorry."

Star squatted down in front of Finn. "I was so worried." She crushed the little boy to her, her heart filled with fear, relief, and something else, love. Love for Finn left her gasping for air. "I didn't know where you were."

"You're hugging me too tight," Finn said, wiggling.

Star let go. She felt tricked. How had she fallen in love with Cade's kids? Had Cade used them as bait to reel her in?

Cade offered her a hand up.

She ignored his hand and stood on her own. "What are you doing here, anyway? You're supposed to be on the boat."

"We limited. The Texans wanted to go hiking on their own, so I came see my new nephew."

Star looked down and realized her hands were shaking.

"Finn, you need to think, little man," Ron said with a shake of his head. "You can't take off like that."

"Sorry," Finn said, looking at Star. His lower lip trembled. Cade took Star's arm. "Come on." He leveled a stern look at Finn. "We'll talk about this more when we get home." Cade's arm moved to Star's shoulders. "Relax. This isn't your fault. Finn runs off all the time. No one can keep track of him, not even me, you know that."

Cade's words, while soothing, didn't change anything. She was growing too attached to Cade and his kids. She didn't want to care that much. Caring hurt.

They all filed inside and took the elevator up. Back in Trudy's room, Star just wanted to escape. From all of them. She didn't want to be responsible for Finn, or for anyone. She needed a valium and a strong martini. No wonder her mother drank.

Losing Finn was Star's cue to get the heck out of Seward. The sooner, the better.

* * *

Cade breathed a sigh of relief when Star's car came into view. His hands gripped the steering wheel. She was here, not headed back for Seattle as he'd feared. Losing Finn had done something to Star, awakened all her reasons for holding him and the kids at arm's length. She'd physically withdrawn from him at the hospital.

When she'd taken off, he'd assumed the worst. It wasn't until he'd driven back to Seward, to Patsy's place, that he'd begun to breathe again. Star's things had still been in the double-wide. He'd waited around for a while, but when she hadn't come home, he'd headed here, to Eagle Ridge.

He'd been right to think she'd hide from him here. And she was hiding, running away from a past she couldn't seem to shake. How did he convince her she'd make a good mother? He had no clue, but he knew he had to try. He'd die inside if she wanted to terminate her pregnancy, if indeed she was pregnant.

Cade exited the truck and started up the path that would take him to the Ridge. Thirty minutes later he found Star, sitting at the edge of the Ridge, her eyes on the canyon and the bay below.

Star turned as he approached. If she was surprised to see him, he couldn't tell. She got to her feet, dusting the dirt from her seat with her hands.

"Hi," he said, searching her face for a clue to her mood but her features remained calm, giving no hint to her mental state.

"You found me." The wind blew a stray hair across her cheek and she brushed it away.

"I thought you might come here."

She cast her eyes toward the canyon. "I feel calm here. The peace clears my head."

"Let's talk about today." He reached for her hand, tugging her around to face him. "About what happened with Finn."

She shook her head. "I'm over it."

"Are you?" He studied her. "Tell me what you're really thinking, Star."

"I'm thinking it's time for me to go home." She reached up, her fingers touching his cheek. "You have to let me go, Cade."

Her words crushed his heart, the ache deep in his chest. "What if I don't want to?"

"I'm not the woman for you. You need a caregiver for the kids, a nurturer. I'm neither of those things."

He stared into her eyes, seeing pain, regret, and love. She loved him, his gut told him that much. His gut also told him he couldn't fix her. She had to fix herself.

"You're wrong," Cade said. "You are both of those things and more, but I'm not going to argue with you. Let's just make the most of the time we have left together, okay?"

Her eyes brightened. "Really? No pressure?"

He drew her to him, his arms sliding around her. "I'm yours for as long as you'll have me. We'll worry about the rest later." He didn't bring up the potential pregnancy, didn't want to rock the boat. Their relationship was as fragile as a spider's web, easily broken.

"Okay," she agreed.

He smiled. "Let's go home. I want to be with you, Star. Nothing else matters."

"In that case," Star said, "I'm all yours."

Cade smiled. Having her with him was enough. For now.

* * *

Star burrowed closer to Cade. They were seated together on the couch in the family room. Around them, the house had grown still. Time was running out for them. They both knew it. Desperation sat with them in the room, wild and reckless.

Star had one night left in Seward, and she wanted to make as many memories as possible to take with her back to Seattle, but privacy was an issue for them.

Cade's hand toyed with her hair. "You've been quiet all night. What are you thinking about?"

"I'm trying not to think at all." She'd helped out at the O'Briens tonight, for the last time. Together, she and Cade had put the twins to bed. Now, the guests had turned in. Ron had arrived home from the hospital, and he'd agreed to keep an eye on the kids so she and Cade could be alone for the last time.

"Let's go to your place," Cade whispered in her ear. "I know you don't like going there, but we need privacy."

The brush of his lips against her skin sent a shiver of desire through Star. More than anything she wanted this last night with him. "I agree."

Cade pulled her up off the couch. Hand in hand, they struck out for Patsy's.

She was sad to leave Alaska; she was excited to go home. And it was her last night with Cade. She didn't want to talk about kids, or parenting, or a possible pregnancy. She only wanted him, had the compelling need to memorize everything about him.

They broke through the trees, the mobile home in view.

"When will you mow it down?" Star asked, a pang of nostalgia stopping her in her tracks.

"Soon. I'd like to get the rubble cleared and the foundation poured as soon as possible."

The mobile home, as run down as it was, was still her home. She'd miss it, and that surprised her. The place meant home, maybe not so much now, but it sure had when she'd been a child. The place was the closest things she had to a childhood home.

"After tomorrow, it's all yours, O'Brien."

Cade put his arm around her, rubbing her shoulders. "Are you sure you're okay?"

She smiled at him. "Fine. Come on. I hope you're going to show me a good time on my last night in town. I need some serious cheering up."

"You're not afraid we'll break another condom?" he asked.

"I don't think fate would be that cruel twice."

She broke away, running up the steps and into the trailer, Cade on her heels. He caught her around the waist, and together they fell onto the couch.

His mouth found hers. Their clothes melted away. They came together fiercely, frantically, as if they couldn't get enough of each other, and maybe they couldn't.

When it was over, and Star was still struggling back to reality, Cade said, "It's a miracle, but the condom held."

"Yeah," Star said, smiling.

Cade kissed her. "I'm going to miss you, Star."

"I'll miss you, too."

"Any chance at all you could find work here?"

The hopeful note in his voice tore at her. "Zero. I've worked my way up the food chain at *Update This!* I'm in line for a big promotion. My life is in the city."

Cade ran his index finger along the curve of her cheek. "I'd never ask you to change your life for me. I did it with Marissa, and it was a mistake. She was never happy here. Maybe we're just too different."

"Maybe we are." Star scooted away from him, a hard ache in her belly. She started to rise, but Cade caught her arm, pulling her back down.

"Don't think tonight, Star," Cade said softly. "I can see the wheels turning. Forget I said anything. Just be with me. I need you. You make me whole. You make me want to be a better man, a better father."

His words cut right through the barbed wire wrapped around her heart. Did she really make him feel those things? Love flooded her heart. For tonight, she'd allow herself to love him back. No thinking. Just for tonight.

He led her down the hall to the bedroom. With great care, Cade laid her on the bed. Taking his time, he made love to her. All of her, every single inch. When he was through, Star had trouble remembering her name, much less why she thought her life was elsewhere.

If Cade were childless, would she find a way to make things work between them?

The question haunted her, continued to haunt her well into the next morning while she wrapped up the rest of Patsy's paintings. She stopped by the post office to ship them to Seattle where she'd go through them at her leisure. She didn't have the heart to tackle the job now. Once she completed that task, she made her goodbyes with Brandi, Bud, and baby Will. Cade and the kids were waiting for her when she finished.

They followed her to the airport, waiting while she dropped off her rental car, then walked with her as far as they could.

"This is it," she said when she had to part from them.

Emma threw her arms around Star, squeezing tight. "Don't go."

Star's heart constricted painfully in her chest. "I have to. Don't forget to daydream."

"I won't," Emma said.

She bent and kissed the little girl, then looked to Finn.

Finn's lip stuck out.

"Let me know if you catch a bird." Star kissed his forehead, then ruffled his hair, and he let her, almost leaning into her caress. "Be good, kiddo."

Emma thrust a package at her. "We made you something, so you won't feel sad when you don't see us anymore."

"Thank you." Star hugged the brightly wrapped gift to her chest, knowing she'd cherish it no matter what it was. "I'm going to miss you guys."

She turned to Brad. "Behave, Brad. No more sneaking out."

"Yeah, right." He gave her a cocky grin.

"Okay, kids." Cade pointed to a bank of nearby chairs. "Wait over there. I have some things to say to Star in private."

Brad ushered the kids away.

"I miss you already," Cade said tightly.

"I miss you, too."

"Call me if you miss your period," Cade said. "I want to know, Star. Promise you'll call."

"I promise." Star rose up on her toes and kissed him. "Goodbye, Cade." She pulled her hands free and took a step away, but he snagged her arm, stopping her. Before she could protest, his mouth took hers, the kiss scattering Star's wits. She clung to him, never wanting to let him go.

Then Cade broke the kiss. Without a word, he left her.

Star touched her lips, watching Cade and the kids until they disappeared from view. With an aching heart, she boarded the plane. Once seated, she opened the package the kids had given her. Inside was a beautiful drawing, a picture of Star, Cade, Finn, Emma, and Brad, standing in front of what could only be their big, Victorian house. Star ran her hand lovingly over the crayon drawing, missing them already. She thought about Cade and the kids the entire way home, and when she got too sad, she made herself think about her job, about the promotion she so wanted.

When she reached her condo, she let herself in, inhaled the scent of the new hardwood floors, the fresh paint, and then promptly burst into tears.

CHAPTER SEVENTEEN

"You did a fabulous job in Alaska," Frank said.

Star tossed her purse in her desk drawer, kicking it closed with a high heel. "Thanks. Did I miss anything good while I was gone?"

"Same old, same old here," Frank said. "Vivienne didn't return home with us from the Fairbanks segment. Rumor is she's with some guy she met at a local bar."

Star bit back a smile. "Really?"

"Yes. Who knew that she'd like the rugged outdoor type?"

"Who knew?" Star agreed, thinking she could say the same for herself. Thinking about Cade sobered her instantly.

Frank gave her a sideways look. "You okay?"

"Sure." She'd never suffered heartache before, but she was pretty sure she had a case of it now. But she'd survive it. She'd survived much worse.

"You seem a little off," Frank said. "Sad."

Star forced a smile. "It wasn't exactly a pleasure trip for me. I had to settle my aunt's estate, remember?"

"Of course I do. Was it hard, going back?"

"Yes and no." Star rifled through a stack of papers on her desk. "When do you leave for Alaska?"

"Sunday morning."

She nodded. "What's next for me?"

"Finish up *Bigger, Bolder, Brighter*, then it's on to a tree house. Up north. Canada."

"A tree house?" Star echoed, intrigued. "Canada? Anywhere near Vancouver?" She thought of her mom and John. Maybe she could visit if they were near the shoot.

"A little more north than that. The tree house is rough. Bare bones. We are going to turn it into something spectacular. You leave two weeks from today."

"Sounds interesting," she said, still thinking about her mom, wondering if she could at least take a side trip through Vancouver.

Frank tossed a file on her desk. "Read up on it. You'll be working with Carrie Shaw on this one."

Carrie Shaw was a favorite designer of Star's. Carrie loved architecture as much as Star did. "Great. I'm looking forward to it."

"Stop by my office after you've had a chance to catch up and we can chat more about the tree house."

"Sounds good. Thanks, Frank."

Star spent the morning sifting through her mail and organizing her desk. Before lunch she downloaded the rest of the pictures from her camera into a file marked Alaska Men.

She clicked through the images, starting with the Fairbanks house, then the Anchorage house, and finally the Seward house. There were three hundred photos of Evan's place.

Frank walked by, poking his head into her office. "Lunch?"

"I'd love some." Star was about to click out of the folder when Frank said, "Are those the Alaska houses?"

"Yes."

"Let me have a peek."

"I've already sent you most of these," Star said, clicking through the images. "Here's Evan's house, see?"

Star clicked. Cade's house filled the screen.

Frank leaned closer. "Wait, what's this?"

"The O'Brien place," Star told him. "They own the land

my aunt's trailer sat on." Star's heart lurched at the thought of Patsy's place no longer sitting on that land.

"More. I want to see more," Frank said, his face lighting up. "This house is fabulous."

"It's a great old Victorian," Star told him, catching his enthusiasm. She'd taken a lot of photos of the house, both exterior and interior.

"Who's that?" Frank asked when a picture of Cade filled the screen.

"Cade O'Brien. He owns the house." A wave of longing hit her full force. Her fingers tightened on the mouse. Was she going to cry? No way.

Star clicked past Cade, neatly erasing him from her mind. She kept clicking. Photos of Emma, Finn, and Brad flashed past. Brandi and Will. More Cade. Destiny, John, Ernie. She didn't want to see any of them.

"You took a lot of pictures of those people," Frank commented.

"Too many." Star exited out of the file. She needed air. "Let's have lunch."

"It's a great house, Star." Frank's forehead creased. "But something tells me it's not the house you love, but the people who live in it."

"Don't read so much into a bunch of photos, Frank." She stood. "Come on. I'm starving."

Frank didn't argue with her, and Star was glad. Because deep down, she knew he was right.

* * *

A little after six p.m. Star left her office and started for home. She'd been home a week now, but today had been the worst. Just knowing that Frank and the rest of the crew had arrived in Seward yesterday had left her with an upset stomach and an exhaustion she hadn't been able to shake the past few days. She craved sleep, needed sleep, making her think her period was due. She often experienced a heavy sleep pattern right before her time of the month. And while this made her happy, she was also distracted, wondering about Evan, the project, and Cade.

Cade had called her, but she hadn't picked up his calls. She wasn't strong enough to hear his voice. What good would it do to foster the connection between them? They had no future.

Star made her way from the car to her condo. Several packages were propped against the front door. The paintings. Her heartbeat picked up. Star opened the door and lugged the four boxes inside. Did she want to open them? She stared at the brown packages so long her eyes went dry. In the end, she couldn't unwrap them. Her fragile psyche kept her from taking the trip down memory lane.

Depressed, Star inhaled, taking in the new smells, needing the scents of her modern condo like an addict needed a drug. These were the smells she loved, new carpet, fresh paint, shiny hardwood. She kicked off her heels and went upstairs to her bedroom.

Star sat on the edge of the bed, then fell backward onto the softness of her new, white duvet cover. Pure heaven. She was home. Home. She willed her mind to go blank and simply absorbed the quiet. No birds singing. No rain hitting the aluminum roof of the double-wide. No kids pestering her. This was the life. The one she wanted.

Her pity party over, Star decided she should probably eat, even though she wasn't really hungry. She got up and slid her aching feet into comfortable slippers. In the kitchen, she opened the freezer and selected a frozen dinner, popping it in the microwave. She'd gained five pounds in Alaska. Her pants were tight. Since returning home, she'd made it a priority to take the weight off.

Ding.

She took the dinner from the microwave, grabbed a fork, and made her way to the couch. Star turned on the TV and took a bite of chicken in orange sauce. She caught the end of a rival design show. The chicken tasted like sawdust in her mouth. Fake food. Not real food like she'd had at Cade's.

What she wouldn't give for some homemade chicken potpie!
Star tossed her fork on top of the uneaten dinner. She
picked up the remote control cruising through the channels,
stopping when a promo for *Update This!* Alaska Men came on.
There they were, her three Alaska guys. Several shots of
Alaska followed. The beauty of the land caught her off guard.
Maybe she was a hometown girl. She missed the place.
Suddenly, busy, overcrowded Seattle didn't seem so great.

Star quickly switched off the TV. Time for her to cowboy-
up. She didn't need any of it, not the space, not the air, and
certainly not the man.

The ring of the phone startled her. Star pressed the talk
button.

"Hello?"

"Star, it's Frank."

"Hey, Frank," she said, sitting back down on the couch.
"How's it going?"

"Not well," Frank barked into the phone. "I need you up
here, now."

"Me?" Star asked, startled by the command. "Why?"

"It's Vivienne. Did you know she was sleeping with our
Seward guy?" Frank didn't give her time to answer. "Well, she
was. Not only that. She broke up with him. He's gone, took
off in that plane of his for parts unknown. Meanwhile, I've
got a crew up here, costing me thousands every day and no
house to update."

"What?" Star struggled to let the news sink in. "What does
Vivienne have to say?"

"Nothing. Not a damned thing. She's missing. She's fired.
I've put up with her French crap long enough."

"Frank, come on," Star said, trying to placate him. "Think.
Can the shoot be put off?"

"No. We're here. That's where you come in."

"Me?" Star said.

"That house. The Victorian. I want to use it and I need
you to make it happen."

"Cade would never go for it, Frank."

"Are you listening to me, Star?" Frank bellowed. "I've already asked him."

Disbelief raced through her, along with a million questions. "What? How? How did you find him?"

"Easy," Frank said. "I just described the house and people gave me directions. This O'Brien fella said okay with one condition, that you're involved. He trusts you, Star."

"No, Frank," Star said, searching her mind for possible excuses. She didn't want to see Cade. Not yet. She was still trying to get over him. "I can't. I have too much work to do here. Plus, renovation takes weeks of pre-production. We don't have the time."

"You're a pro," Frank said. "You can piece things together quickly. You know the area, the businesses. Hotel and catering are done. Dump the rest of your work on Suzy. Vivienne is out. Carrie Shaw is in. I've booked a nine a.m. flight for you both. Filming will be delayed until Wednesday to get you both up to speed. Get Carrie all the photos you have of the kitchen. I don't care if the two of you have to stay up all night, but when you get here tomorrow, I want a design done. You can help Carrie. You know the family, know their tastes."

"Frank that kind of design takes time," Star protested.

"This could mean a promotion for you, Star. Flight. Nine a.m. Do I make myself clear?"

"Yes, Frank," Star said, her mind stuck on the word *promotion*. "I'll call Carrie right now."

"I knew I could count on you, Star."

The line went dead.

Holy smoke. A possible promotion. She was going back to Alaska. Her stomach did a funny jump. Cade had asked for her, the rat. She was going to see him. The kids. Trudy, Ron, and Daniel. Brandi, Bud, and Will.

But to what end? More heartache when she had to leave them for the second time?

Star glanced over at the picture on her fridge—the one Emma had drawn of her, Cade, and the kids. She got up. At the fridge, she flipped the drawing over, pinning it back on with the magnet. The blank page stared back at her. Clean and neat, just like her life.

Satisfied, she picked up the phone and punched in Carrie's number.

* * *

Star stared out the window of the rented SUV watching the rain run in rivulets down the glass. She glanced over at their driver, Bill. He'd picked them up from the airport, and he didn't look any happier about the crummy weather than she did. Traffic had been terrible due to a rollover accident just outside of Anchorage. The delay had added an extra hour to their drive.

Her stomach fluttered as the SUV made the turn into Cade's driveway. It was almost four p.m. Would he be home? Or would he be out fishing? She'd spent the entire morning imagining how their meeting would go. Would he be aloof? Would he hug her? Kiss her?

"There it is," Carrie said from the back seat. "It's gorgeous. The outside could use a little TLC, too. I'll have to think about that."

Star devoured the house with her eyes. To her, the place looked like home. Vehicles were parked everywhere. A sign on the front lawn said *Update This! Alaska Men*. Members of the crew milled around, some using oversized orange and blue umbrellas stamped with the *Update This!* logo, a big U atop a T. A large tent had been set up on the front lawn to house their big carpentry equipment and to give the crew shelter from the driving rain.

She didn't see any of the O'Briens. Not even Snowbell. They were probably huddled inside next to the fireplace.

Frank spotted them, an umbrella in hand; he broke away from a group of men, striding toward them. Her boss was in high gear, wearing the stressed out scowl he reserved for when they were about to go to tape.

The SUV stopped. Star and Carrie exited the vehicle. Star

reached back inside for her purse and her laptop.

"Thank God you're here," Frank thundered. He took Star's arm, pulling her under the umbrella with him. "Why didn't you tell me it's so wet here it's like a cow peeing on a flat rock?" Before she could reply, he said, "O'Brien isn't the easiest guy to work with. I need you, Star. March right in there and smooth things over with him. He's dragging his feet, waiting for you. I don't know what he's got to be upset about. We've compensated him for his loss of income. He's sittin' pretty, damn it."

"Calm down, Frank," Star said, frowning. "I tried to warn you." She glanced around. "Besides, I don't see Cade's truck. Is he even here?"

"He's here. His kid took the truck."

Star smiled. "Brad? The grounding must be over."

"I don't give a rat's patutie about the kid," Frank said. "Time is money, Star. Go and use your wiles on O'Brien. The guy looks like he hasn't been laid in years."

"Gee, Frank," Star said dryly, "I didn't know you were my boss and my pimp."

"Oh, crap. I guess that wasn't exactly a PC comment." Frank gave her a twisted smile. "Sorry. Will you please go in and talk to O'Brien?"

"Sure."

"Carrie," Frank shouted, as if the designer were across a football field instead of three feet away. "Let's see what you've got. It better be good or this guy will walk and we'll be hung out like wet, and I do mean *wet*, laundry on a hot summer day."

Frank left her in the rain. Star started for the house. Before she reached the door it opened and Emma and Finn ran out.

"Star!" Emma cried.

"Star," Finn echoed.

The kids mobbed her, throwing their arms around her, jumping up and down.

"Hey, you two," Star said, her hands cupping their heads.

And it wasn't enough. She needed more of them. Star squatted, taking them into her arms, inhaling their kid scent: baby shampoo and fresh air. "I've missed you guys."

"We missed you, too, Star," Emma said.

"It's not as fun without you," Finn told her. "Trudy's busy all the time. And the baby cries and cries."

Emma nodded. "He does, Star. He's real loud."

Star smiled, then laughed, a strange lightness invading her spirit. "I guess he's doing what he's supposed to do. Come on, let's get inside. I'm soaked, and so are you."

She stood, and they ran into the house. "Is your dad here?" she asked when they were in the foyer.

Emma nodded. "He's in the kitchen talking to some men."

Star shrugged out of her wet coat and hung it on the coat rack. Quickly, she ran a hand over her hair, but feared she looked a little like a drowned rat—and she wanted to thank Frank for the image. Even she was starting to think in idioms.

"Come on." Emma tugged on Star's hand.

Finn ran ahead. "Dad. Star's back."

Star let Emma pull her down the hall and into the kitchen.

Cade stood with Ed and Buck, two of the carpenters. He must have heard Finn because he turned away from the men. Her eyes met his, and for Star, everything else stopped.

"Star's here," Emma said in a singsong voice. "See, Daddy?"

"I see," Cade said, his eyes on her.

Her heart began to beat again. Joy filled her chest. Was this what love felt like? She wanted to touch him, to kiss him, and even that wouldn't be enough. Heaven help her, she'd missed him. She hadn't realized how much until this moment. Her emotions felt raw, exposed, and she wasn't sure how to conceal them from Cade.

"Will you excuse us?" Cade said to Ed and Buck without taking his eyes off Star.

"Sure," Ed said, exchanging a knowing look with Buck.

Buck followed Ed from the room.

"Star," Ed said as he passed.

Buck gave her a nod.

"Finn, Emma, will you leave us alone for a minute?" Cade asked.

"Aww, do we have to?" Finn grumbled.

"I want to be with, Star," Emma said, stomping her little foot.

"Wait in the other room," Cade said in an authoritative tone. "Just for a minute. I promise."

"Come on, Finn," Emma said, but Finn didn't budge. She tugged on his shirt. "Daddy said."

That made Finn move and he trailed after his sister.

Star could hear the tick of the clock on the wall. Her heart thundered in her chest.

"Hey," she said softly, feeling sixteen again, shy and self-conscious.

"You don't pick up my calls." He walked toward her, sexy, rugged, and pure man.

"How are Trudy and the baby?" she asked, avoiding his question.

"Great. They're upstairs." He reached for her. A thin line of sexual attraction separated them.

"Asking for me was a dirty trick," she said not sure if she wanted him to touch her. If he did, he'd win. She couldn't resist him and they both knew it.

"It got you back here. Welcome home."

She opened her mouth to tell him her home was in Seattle, but before she could speak, he took her face in his hands and kissed her.

A dam of emotion burst inside her. Unable to help herself, Star moved into him, opening her mouth, taking his essence, his taste, inside her. Her palms flattened against his chest, then moved around his torso, reveling in the feel of his muscular body under the soft cotton of his T-shirt.

"Make out on your own time," Frank growled. "We've got a show to do."

They broke apart. Star's wits totally scattered.

"My fault," Cade said with a grin.

Frank leveled a let's get down to business look at her. "Let's get this show on the road. Carrie!"

Carrie hustled into the kitchen, her arms full of samples.

"Show Mr. O'Brien what we have in store for him," Frank ordered.

"Happy to," Carrie said brightly. She went to the breakfast bar and set down the samples, then turned to Cade. "Hi, I'm Carrie Shaw, your designer." She extended her hand to Cade and he took it. "I have a lot to show you."

"I'm Cade O'Brien." He joined her at the counter.

"Star had a lot of input," Carrie said. "I hope we're on target with your vision for the room." Carrie opened a book containing floor samples. "Here's what we came up with. We want to modernize your kitchen, of course, but we want to do it in a way that stays true to the Victorian home. So yes, we are going to update, but we are also going to replicate, and by that, I mean we are going to stay true to the original kitchen. For instance, your sink. You have a farm sink, probably last updated in the 1950s. Here's a photo of the sink I'd like to use. It's modern, beautiful, but modeled after an old farm sink. See the design?" She pointed to the scroll pattern on the front of the sink. "It's gorgeous."

Cade watched as Carrie laid out the design, showing him colors, appliances, floor samples. While the designer talked, Star watched Cade. When he'd seen everything, he looked at Star.

"What do you think?" he asked, motioning her over.

"It doesn't matter what I think," Star said. "What do you think? It's your house."

"I'm fine with the house the way it is," he said. "I want to know if you like it."

"Why?" she asked, wondering what he was up to. Did he think he could lure her here permanently with a pretty new kitchen and hot kisses? Not happening.

She was about to tell him so when Frank said, "Just answer the question, Star," in a tone that said, love it or lose your job.

"I love it, Cade," she said. "I think the design is perfect for the house."

"Perfect," Cade said to Frank. "Let's get started."

CHAPTER EIGHTEEN

"I can't believe how much he's grown in a little over a week." Star rocked baby Daniel in her arms. "He's got the dark O'Brien hair. He looks just like his daddy."

Trudy smiled. "I know."

Trudy's face shone with love for her son, making Star wonder how she'd feel about her own child if she were pregnant. Was she capable of that kind of love? Baby love was powerful, all consuming. How did one survive such an emotion? Star had no idea, but she did know that loving the baby wouldn't be her problem. No, the problem came with having to raise a child.

"You look great, Trudy," Star said, meaning it.

"Thanks." Form-fitting black jeans cupped Trudy's backside. A pink T-shirt hugged breasts heavy with mother's milk. "I'm glad you're here, Star. We've all missed you."

"It's only been a week," Star reminded her. But it seemed like forever.

"I know. Still, it's not the same without you. I'm selfish enough to want you here all the time. I loved having another woman close by." She sighed. "But I understand why you won't stay. Your life is exciting and glamorous. All these television people. It's so fun to watch them work. And the kitchen, well, you know how excited I am about that. More so now that Cade has decided against expanding. I'll be cooking in that brand new kitchen every day."

"What do you mean?" Star asked. "Has Cade given up the idea of building over at Patsy's place?"

"Didn't he tell you?" Trudy's eyebrows rose in question. "He hasn't knocked down the mobile home. My theory is that he couldn't bear to once you left. He knows the place means something to you."

Star digested the news, not sure what to think.

"He's fallen for you, Star," Trudy said. "I can tell. He's not the same. You changed him."

"It can't work between us," Star said sadly. "We live in different states. We want different things."

"Can't you find a middle ground?"

Star shook her head. "I don't see how. I can't give up my career to raise a family. I don't want to."

"But you love the kids now. I can tell," Trudy said. "And I even think that Brad has grown on you." She laughed. "Well, as much as a teenager with a gigantic attitude can."

"They're great kids," Star agreed, "but they're still kids. I do love them, but they need a mother, a full-time mother."

"Speaking of that," Trudy said. "Cade is going to hire a nanny. I have my hands super-full with Daniel and my work at the B & B. We need help."

Star hated the thought of a nanny, but on the flipside, Cade did need the help. Hiring a nanny was the responsible thing to do.

"Are the kids okay with that?" Star asked.

Trudy shrugged. "Who knows? It won't be so bad. I'll be right here to make sure things go smoothly."

"I guess so," Star said, feeling oddly bereft.

"Brandi and Bud are here," Cade said as he came into the room.

Star passed Daniel back to Trudy. She'd called Brandi earlier and invited her over. After wrapping for the day, the crew had gone to their hotel. She was the only one staying at the O'Briens. Tomorrow they were going to begin demolition. At that time, Trudy and Ron were taking the kids to stay at her parents' place in town.

They had one week to get the kitchen done. *Update This!* worked at a break-neck pace.

One week in Seward.

One week with Cade.

"Go ahead," Trudy said. "I need to change Daniel."

"Okay."

"How are you holding up?" Cade asked, his fingers closing around hers.

"I'm doing fine," Star said. "It's so good to visit with Trudy, but this isn't real, Cade, you know that, right? I'm not staying forever."

"I know," Cade said. "But I don't have to like it."

When they hit the hall, Star could hear Brandi even before she could see her, and then they were hugging, baby Will between them.

"Give me that baby," Star said, taking Will from Brandi. Star kissed his cheek. "You are so handsome, Will." Will opened his little mouth and tried to gum Star's chin.

"Looks just like his daddy," Bud joked, leaning in to kiss Star's cheek.

"I could eat you up," Star said to Will. She kissed him again.

"Looks like you really missed him," Brandi said in a knowing tone. Will made a darling, cooing sound and they all laughed. "Guess he missed you, too."

"We all missed Star," Cade said.

Star glanced up. She could tell Cade liked seeing her with a baby in her arms.

Unsettled, Star handed Will back to Brandi. "Come on," she said. "Let's find a place where we can sit and talk."

Star headed for the back door, but she didn't miss the look of compassion—or was it pity?—that passed between her sister and Cade.

A look that bruised Star's heart.

* * *

"Come with me."

Cade held his hand out to Star. He was finally free to enjoy her, make love to her like he wanted to.

They were alone. Brandi and Bud had taken a sleeping baby Will home. Trudy and Ron were upstairs with Daniel. Emma and Finn were in bed. Brad was out on a date.

Cade's fingers closed around Star's, her skin soft and warm against his. He pulled her up from the lawn chair.

"Where are we going?" she asked.

"There's a hammock out here with our name on it."

Star smiled. "Is it big enough for two?"

"Who cares?" He grinned.

Cade swung himself into the hammock, holding it steady while Star climbed in. The hammock tipped, but Cade caught Star, pulling her close, gathering her softness to him. She snuggled against him, fit to him like she was made for him. Man, he never wanted to let her go. He'd missed her like crazy last week. How could he convince her to stay? How did he erase years of damage and heartache? His arms tightened around her.

Her hand moved across his ribcage, her touch light, exploratory.

"I'm beat," she said.

"Me, too. Your boss is exhausting." But he didn't care. He'd put up with a hundred Franks to have Star near. He knew he was crazy to lure her back here, but he'd been unable to help himself. He needed her in a way he'd never needed Marissa. Star was a part of him, had been a part of him forever. First love, forever love.

"Isn't he?" Star agreed. "I thought it was just me, but Frank wears everyone out."

Cade shifted so they were facing each other, their bodies touching everywhere. He kissed her forehead, her nose, her mouth. Her sweet taste fueled him, made him ache for her.

Star kissed him back. They kissed, and kissed, and kissed

some more until they were totally lost in each other. Cade's hands found their way under her shirt and Star moaned.

"You're so soft," he said. "I love touching you."

"I want to be naked with you, O'Brien."

Cade smiled. "The mobile home is still there."

"I wanted to talk to you about that."

"Later." He didn't want to explain why he couldn't demolish the place. Even he didn't fully understand why. He only knew the trailer was part of the woman he loved, and if that scared her, well, too bad.

Star laughed as he pulled her from the hammock.

Like two lovesick teenagers, they ran down the path to Patsy's. Once inside, they stripped each other naked. Their lovemaking was fierce, the sex so hot, Cade knew he had to find a way to convince her to stay. Being without Star was not an option. She might be a city girl, but her heart was here, with him.

They belonged together.

He'd always known that; now he just had to convince her.

* * *

They were on day four of the shoot when Vivienne pulled into Cade's driveway, driving Evan Jenson's pickup truck.

Needing some time away from the constant hammering and sawing, Star had just returned from a walk. The weather had cleared and blue sky stretched overhead as far as she could see. To her left, the show's carpenters worked, building what, Star wasn't sure.

Star paused on the front porch, waiting for the designer to join her.

"Star, *bonjour!*" Vivienne called as she jumped down from the driver's seat. "What are you doing here?"

"Don't ask," Star said. "Where have you been? With Evan? I recognize his truck."

"Guilty." Vivienne smiled. She placed her hand on her heart. "I'm in love."

Star's eyes narrowed. "I thought you two had a fight."

"We made up." Vivienne's eyebrows rose suggestively. "Makeup sex is great."

"I hope Evan was worth it," Star said. "Frank says you're fired."

"Evan *is* worth it." Vivienne held out her left hand. A large diamond ring circled her ring finger. "We got married."

"What?" Star asked incredulous. "You barely know him. What's wrong with you? You don't get married on a whim. Trust me. My mother's done it five times."

"When it is right, you know," Vivienne said in a dreamy tone.

"That's what my mother always says and she's trolling for husband number six."

"You're too cynical, Star. Believe in the fairytale. So what if your mother's been married five times? That's five times she's fallen in love. Falling in love is fabulous. You should try it."

"Are you in love?" Star asked. "Really in love?"

The smile slid from Vivienne's face. "Of course I am."

"You know I wish you well," Star said, not wanting to totally crush Vivienne's happiness. "I only wish you'd given the relationship more time. You know?"

"You will never change." Vivienne's jaw set in a stubborn line. "On a scale of one to ten how mad is Frank?"

"He's a fifteen."

Vivienne gave Star a tight smile. "Ouch. Where is the old grouch?"

"Inside, telling everyone what to do."

"So exactly where do you fit in here?" Vivienne asked. "Cade's house is a stand-in for Evan's place, yes?"

"Yes. Cade would only consent to the remodel if I came along."

"Is that so?" Vivienne smiled. "Maybe you're not as immune to love as you pretend to be. Well, wish me luck."

"Good luck," Star said, knowing Vivienne would need more than luck on her side. Frank could be tough. He wouldn't cave easily. If Vivienne wanted her job back, she was going to have to grovel, and even then there was no guarantee Frank would give in.

Cade appeared in the doorway. "Hey."

"Hi." She smiled. Just looking at him lightened her spirit. There was no mistaking the chemistry between them. When Cade came into the room, Star's world got brighter.

"Do you have time for coffee?" he asked.

"My stomach's bothering me today," she said, "but I will take a cup of tea. I think Frank is giving me an ulcer."

She followed Cade inside to the family room, where a makeshift kitchen had been set up. Star filled a mug with hot water from the food service cart and added a tea bag.

"Your stomach?" Cade asked, taking a sip of his coffee. "You'd tell me if your period was late, right?"

Star looked at him as if he were crazy. "My period is not going to be late. I know my body. The premenstrual signs are there, the bloating, the exhaustion. I'm crabby."

"Still," Cade said, "you'd tell me, right?"

"Of course."

"I know the thought of being a parent terrifies you, but it doesn't scare me. As much as I want you in my life, I'll take the baby without you."

"Are you saying you'd want me to carry the baby to term, then just walk away?" Star asked, incredulous.

"That would be your choice," Cade said. "It's not what I want. If you are pregnant, I want us to raise the baby together."

Star remembered the feel of Will's kick when he'd been inside Brandi. To feel the baby inside her, to nurture it, to bring it into the world, she couldn't walk away and leave the baby with Cade, could she?

"I don't want a baby," she said, the words low, for his ears only. "You know that. I'm not pregnant."

"I don't want a baby either," Cade said, "but if you are pregnant, we have to deal with it."

Star set her tea down on the table. "Stop it. We're talking about something that hasn't happened yet."

"Okay," Cade said, his tone gentler now. "Okay. But I want you to know I'm here for you."

Star nodded. She didn't reply, she couldn't. Her insides were in a knot. Her period was a day late. A day. Not out of the norm for her. She could count on being a day or two early or late most months. Yet, she didn't confide in Cade. She refused to freak out.

She was in line for a promotion. Her life was on track, perfect. There was no room for a baby, no room for Cade, or his kids. She didn't want a baby. Not now, not ever.

* * *

Later that afternoon, Star found Frank in the living room where he was watching Bret Parker, the host of *Update This!* do an on-air interview with Cade.

Her boss stood out of camera range, his arms folded across his chest. His brows were drawn together, and Star could see the tension on his face. He hadn't calmed down yet. His fight with Vivienne still bothered him. Vivienne was still fired, but Star thought Frank would hire her back eventually. She was too good, too much of a ratings favorite.

Star watched Cade. He sat on the couch, a camera in his face. She stayed in the doorway, out of the shot. Frank noticed her and put his hand up, palm out, the gesture telling her to stay put.

"It's the end of day four," Bret said to Cade. "How do you think it's going?"

"Fine." Cade's forehead creased. "It's not easy to watch the place being torn apart, but everyone seems to know what they're doing."

"You don't sound like you have a lot of faith in the team," Bret said, goading Cade, no doubt hoping for a negative reaction.

"Time will tell," Cade replied, keeping his cool.

"I guess it will," Bret agreed. "What do you think of the colors, now that the walls are painted?"

"I'm not sure about all the red," Cade said. "The color is

strong."

"It is," Bret agreed. "Do you have anything to say to Carrie? It's her design after all."

"I trust her," Cade said, looking directly at Star.

She gave him a small smile.

"Have you given any thought to how you'll respond when the mail from the female viewers comes pouring in? A widower like you, three adorable kids, the ladies are going to eat you up."

"Not really," Cade said, and Star knew he'd agreed to play along with the single guy looking for a wife premise the show was based on, but he had no intention of following through, and Frank let him get away with no dates, in exchange for using the house.

"You're a good looking guy," Bret said. "You're going to get more offers than you can imagine."

"I guess I'll think about that when the time comes."

"A good diplomatic answer," Bret said, giving the camera the dimpled grin that had earned him a female following of his own.

Cade nodded.

"Well, you heard him, folks," Bret said directly to the camera. "Cade's willing to trust our team. Let's just hope they don't let him down."

Bret made a cutting motion with his hand.

"We're out," Frank said before turning to Cade. "Good job, Cade. Just the right amount of doubt and mystery. Viewers love that."

Cade stood. "Glad I could help." He started for Star.

She met him halfway. "You're a natural on camera."

Cade grimaced. "I doubt that. I was uncomfortable."

"It didn't show. Besides, viewers expect you to be uncomfortable. They know you're not an actor."

Frank joined them. "You've done a great job, Star."

"Thanks, Frank." Star glanced away from Cade to her clipboard. "We're right on schedule. The demolition is complete. The painting is done. The plumber is nearly finished, and the floor guys are about to go in and put in the new sub-floor."

"No, I mean it," Frank said with a bob of his head. "You rose to the challenge on this one. I've been watching you for a while now, wondering if you were producer material. You have to be tough, a leader. I think you have what it takes, kid. You've proven that by being my anytime, anywhere, anything gal."

Star snapped to attention, her stomach tightening in anticipation. Was this finally it? Was he promoting her?

"I can do the job," she said. "You know I can. I'm dedicated. I work hard. Work comes first for me. It always has and always will."

She didn't glance at Cade, didn't want to see his reaction to their conversation.

"I know that, Star," Frank said, "that's why I've decided to promote you to associate producer."

Star grinned. "Really, Frank?" A giddiness overtook her, a high better than champagne.

"The job is yours. Of course, you'll be spending more time in the field. Your hours will be longer. Your responsibilities greater. Can you handle all that?"

"You know I can."

Frank nodded. "Good enough. You can start with the tree house project. It'll be your baby. As soon as we wrap here, you can take off for Canada."

"Thank you!" Star said, her excitement bubbling over.

Frank smiled. "You earned it, kid." He walked away, then yelled, "Bret, quit making eyes at Carrie and get your butt in the kitchen."

Still smiling, Star turned to Cade.

"Congratulations." Cade smiled, but to Star the smile looked forced.

"Thanks. This is my dream job, Cade," she said, wanting him to understand how important this promotion was to her. "I'm finally getting everything I ever wanted."

"Are you, Star?" Cade asked softly.

She stiffened. "Yes."

He glanced away from her, and she knew he was upset. "And if you're pregnant?"

"I've never misrepresented myself to you," she said gently.

He frowned. "I know that. I'm just sorry."

"For what?"

"For everything."

Her fingers tightened on the clipboard. "What do you mean?"

"Star," Frank yelled from the other room. "I need you."

"You better go," Cade said with a sad shake of his head. "After all, you're on the clock."

Before Star could reply, Cade left her standing there alone. Damn him. He'd managed to steal the joy from her promotion. Star lifted her chin. He could only steal her joy if she let him. Her shoulders squared, Star wheeled around and headed for Frank, and the job that made her so happy.

* * *

Cade felt guilty, and he didn't like the feeling.

But damn it, something had happened between him and Star, something he didn't want to lose. He didn't understand how a career could come first, not when it came to two people being together, especially not when there was a possibility Star could be pregnant. If he could do his job in Seattle, would he consider moving for her? He didn't know. He'd have to uproot the kids. His leaving would affect Ron and Trudy. So many people depended on him. Even so, he was willing to compromise, to find a way they could be together. There had to be a middle ground and if he didn't want to lose her, he needed to figure out where it was.

He'd done everything he could think of to make her happy, even consenting to this kitchen makeover. What did she want? Could he ever make her happy, or had her ugly childhood damaged her beyond repair? What would it take for Star to realize where her heart really belonged?

Cade let himself out the back door. He pulled up a deck

chair and sat. The evening air buzzed with nature's sounds, and yet an odd quiet crowded the space. He missed Finn, Emma, and Brad. He needed his kids like he needed air. He couldn't imagine his life without them. Or without Star.

Upstairs, she was taking a bath, a bath he'd wanted to join her in, but he wasn't sure he'd be welcome. He'd tried to be happy for her when Frank gave her the promotion, but he'd failed. She'd seen right through his words. He'd been so disappointed.

The back door creaked. Ron came down the stairs, pulling up a chair beside him.

"Hey," Ron said. "Things are looking good."

"I didn't know you were here."

"In and out," Ron said, leaning back in the chair. "Trudy sent me for Emma's pink blanket. I'm heading right back."

"Kiss the kids for me."

"I will." Ron smiled. "Trudy is tickled with the remodel."

"I'm glad she likes it," Cade said. "It's too red for my taste."

Ron shrugged. "I don't care what color it is. If Trudy's happy, I'm happy."

When Cade didn't comment, Ron said. "What's up? You look like you just lost your best friend."

"Star got promoted." Cade frowned. "She leaves for Canada as soon as this show is in the can."

"It's what she wants, right?" Ron asked.

Cade nodded.

"You've really fallen for her, haven't you?"

Cade sighed. "Yeah."

Ron smiled. "It's always been her, hasn't it?"

"Yep."

"You need to fight for Star," Ron said. "Find a way to make it work."

"How?" Cade held up his hands. "My work is here, hers is there. Then there's the issue of kids. Star doesn't want any. I have three. The woman I'm with needs to want my kids. They've already had a mother they couldn't count on. I won't do that to them again."

"Star's family phobic," Ron said. "Trudy told me. Star's afraid to care too much. She's taken a beating when it comes to responsibility. She's tired of being the glue that holds everything together. You've got to be her glue, Cade. Get it?"

"Her glue?" Cade asked, thinking his brother was becoming more like Trudy every day.

"Show her what teamwork's all about. She wouldn't have to raise the kids alone. You're there for her, man. We all are."

Cade stood. "You didn't really come here for the blanket, did you?"

Ron shrugged. "You have the place to yourself tonight and tomorrow night, after that she'll be gone. Figure things out, bro." Ron patted Cade's shoulder before rising. "See you tomorrow."

"Yeah, tomorrow." Cade waited until he heard the sound of Ron's truck starting before he went inside. He wanted to be with Star, wanted to show her he could be her glue.

When he reached Star's room, he let himself in. The bed was empty, the room quiet. Light came from the adjoining bathroom.

Cade walked to the bathroom. In the doorway, he stopped. Star was in the tub, up to her neck in bubbles. She had all her hair pinned up on her head. Her eyes were closed.

She looked like an angel.

She sensed him, her eyes opening.

"I knocked," he said.

She reached up, and with a bubbled covered hand she pulled the ear buds from her ears. "What?"

"I said, I knocked, but obviously you didn't hear me."

She tossed the ear buds on a nearby chair, where they landed near her iPod. "Is everyone gone?"

Cade nodded. They needed to talk, but seeing her in the tub made him switch gears. More than anything, he wanted to crawl into that big claw footed tub with her. They could talk later.

Cade pulled his shirt up over his head and tossed it on the

chair.

Star's eyes widened.

He unbuckled his belt, and unbuttoned his jeans.

Star smiled.

Cade sat on the edge of the chair and pulled his boots off, then his socks. He stood, facing her, and pushed his jeans down, stepping out of them.

"I guess you're happy to see me." Star laughed softly.

Cade already had his boxers off. "I guess I am."

She sat up, making room for him as he got in the tub with her, sliding in behind her.

Cade leaned back in the tub, his head on the rim. Star settled back against him, her head on his chest, her back against his stomach. Cade's arms went around her, his hands finding her breasts.

The water was cold and all over the floor when Cade finished loving Star.

It was a bath neither of them would ever forget.

CHAPTER NINETEEN

Cramps woke Star. The kind of cramps that could only mean one thing—she had her period. Yet, she didn't move, not right away.

Beside her, Cade slept and having him in bed with her made a reality of every fantasy she'd ever had. The morning light played over his features, and she resisted the urge to touch the delicate skin above his upper lip, trace his cheek, kiss his mouth.

Last night had been magical. Cade's tenderness with her tugged on her heartstrings, making her wish things were different for them.

Star rolled over and looked her fill of him. Boy, was she going to miss him when she left, but leaving was the right thing to do. She truly believed that. She'd worked long and hard for this promotion. No person in her right mind would give up an opportunity like this. Cade stirred, rolling over, away from her. Star sat up. When Cade didn't move, she got out of bed and headed for the bathroom. She shut the door behind her, but didn't push it all the way closed, not wanting to risk waking Cade. She sat on the toilet and checked for signs of her period, but she didn't see anything. Not yet, but maybe later today.

"Star?"

"Just a minute. I'm using the bathroom."

"Oh, sorry."

Star finished up. She flushed the toilet, then washed up at the sink.

When she exited the bathroom, Cade was sitting on the edge of the bed. He rose, then went into the bathroom and shut the door.

Star got back into bed, wondering if they had time for a little morning sex before the crew arrived. She smiled. Waking up with Cade was fun. The toilet flushed. Water ran, for a long time. How long did it take for Cade to wash his hands? She glanced at the clock. They were wasting precious time.

The door opened, and Cade made his way to the bed. He sat down on the edge and said, "We need to talk."

Serious worry lines creased his forehead. Star rolled to her back, not wanting to have another conversation about her career or a possible pregnancy right now. She felt too good, too relieved, too sated.

Cade looked at her. "I'd feel better if you took a pregnancy test. Enough time has passed, right? I've done the calculations. The possible pregnancy is like an elephant between us. I want to know, don't you?"

She nodded, resigning herself to the conversation. "I have cramps. I'm sure my period is about to start."

"But if it doesn't start today? Come on, Star, I have a stake in this, too." Cade's jaw tightened. "I'd like to know for sure before you leave."

"Okay," she said, seeing no way around his request. "If I don't have my period by the end of today, I'll get a test. Will that work for you?"

He nodded.

Outside, car doors slammed. The crew was beginning to arrive. Darn. No morning sex.

"Time for work," Star said with regret.

"Yeah," Cade agreed, moving aside so she could get up.

* * *

Star set the pregnancy test kit on the coffee table.

Day five of the renovation was over. The crew was gone for the day. The kids, Ron, Trudy, and Daniel were staying in town again tonight.

And Cade was nowhere in sight.

Star took a seat on the couch. So far, no period, and worse, her cramps had stopped. She hated to admit it, but she was starting to freak out. No way did she want a baby, not even with Cade. She refused to let her mind wander down the path to parenthood. She simply couldn't go there.

Where the heck was Cade? She wanted to take the test with him, wanted to include him.

The sound of an approaching vehicle pulled Star from the couch. She went to the front door and opened it.

Cade slammed the truck door and walked toward her. He waved when he saw her. As usual, her heart sped up at the sight of him. Her hand went to her stomach. Did she carry his baby? If she did, she had some hard decisions to make.

"Hi," she said when he was close enough to hear her.

He came up the steps. "Did you get your period?"

She frowned. "It's nice to see you, too," she said sarcastically. She didn't even know if she was pregnant, and she already felt like the baby was coming between them.

"Sorry," he offered. "I'm wound up, you know?"

"I know." She went inside. He followed. Star pointed to the coffee table, to the test kit. "Come with me while I take it."

Cade took her hand, giving her fingers a light squeeze of encouragement. "Let's go."

Star retrieved the test and hand in hand they went upstairs. In the bathroom, she sat on the toilet and took the stick from the box. Cade sat down on the rim of the tub.

She couldn't pee.

"Could you turn around or something?" she asked. "Shy bladder."

"Fine."

Cade stood and gave her his back.

Star peed on the stick. She carefully set the stick on the counter before fastening her pants.

Cade had already turned around. "How long does it take?"

"It's supposed to be pretty fast."

Cade looked at his watch.

Star was afraid to look at the test.

For a full minute they stood there, three feet apart, not moving, the tension between them as thick as spring mud.

"I can't stand it." Cade peered at the stick. "There's a line."

Star leaned in. "A line means not pregnant."

Cade straightened. "That should make you a very happy woman."

Star smiled, sweet relief filling her. "If it's true. Let's give it ten minutes."

"Okay."

For ten minutes they barely spoke. When Cade said, "Time," Star picked up the stick. Not pregnant. She held the stick out to Cade.

"Whew, that's a relief," Cade said.

"You seem more relieved than I do," Star said, melancholy settling inside her. She should be rejoicing. They should be celebrating. After all, it was their last night together.

"Maybe I am," Cade said. "I wasn't looking forward to raising a baby on my own."

"Oh," Star said, oddly bereft. "That makes sense."

"Are you okay?" Cade touched her face, rubbing his thumb against her cheek. "This is what you wanted, right?"

"Right," she said a bit too quickly.

"You can leave here free and clear," Cade reminded her. "Unless of course, you want to change your mind. I'm willing to do whatever it takes to have you in my life."

Star's heart melted. She didn't deserve him. "I wish I could be the woman you want," she said, his kindness torturing her. "But I can't."

"I love you," Cade said, the words hanging in the air

between them.

"Love isn't enough," Star replied sadly. "Not for me."

"So this is it? We're going to end things now?" Cade asked, a hitch in his voice. "Is that what you really want, Star?"

Star turned away from him. She couldn't look at him, couldn't bear to see the pain in his eyes. "I think it's best."

He didn't reply. When she gathered the courage to turn and face him, he was gone. A few seconds later, his truck roared to life.

An unbearable ache formed in Star's chest. She had nothing to apologize for or feel guilty about. Nothing. She'd always been honest with Cade.

So why did it hurt to breathe, to think?

She knew the answer. She'd never be the same because Cade had managed to touch her heart in a way she'd never thought possible.

The problem was she was too scared to love him back.

* * *

The following afternoon, Cade found himself in the kitchen, a kitchen that would forever remind him of Star. His gut ached when he thought of the way he'd left things between them, but their breakup was for the best. They'd never see eye to eye when it came to family. Star was too messed up inside.

Yet, she'd left her stamp both in his kitchen and on his heart. The crew was gone. There were no cameras. No chatty talk show host to deal with. Most importantly, Star was gone, and as much as he hated to admit it, she'd left a hole in his life. Damn. He regretted walking away last night. If he'd gone back to her, could he have persuaded her to stay, to give their relationship another try? Probably not. The only one who could make things work between them was Star. She had to accept him for what he was, both a lover and a father. He was scared of making the wrong choices, too, but he knew with certainty that Star was worth the risk. Until Star was willing to take a risk of her own, they had no future.

Trudy and Ron came into the room. His sister-in-law's face lit up as she looked around.

"I love it, I love it, I love it," Trudy gushed. She twirled in a circle. "I can't get enough of this room. It smells new. And look at the granite." Trudy ran her hand over the smooth black counter top.

Trudy was right. The new kitchen gleamed. The black and white floor was so clean you could eat off of it. The white walls made the room seem twice as bright, and Cade had to admit the red accent wall really did pull the whole room together.

"It really is beautiful," Ron said, exchanging grins with his wife. "What do you think, Cade?"

"I'm glad it's over."

Trudy's face fell. "Do you want to talk about Star?"

"No." Cade made his way to the back door and let himself out.

"Cade, wait," Trudy called.

The screen door banged shut behind him. He didn't want to talk about Star with anybody. He couldn't. He loved her too much.

Cade sank down on the steps, his head in his hands. He loved her.

He wanted all of her. He didn't want a part-time wife, or a part-time mother for his kids. He didn't want a woman who freaked out at the thought of having his child. He didn't want that kind of woman at all, but that was the woman he'd fallen in love with. What the heck was he supposed to do about that?

Nothing. Nada. Zip. He'd done it. He'd let her go.

There was no future for them. All he had left was the bright, shiny kitchen, a glaring reminder of their time together.

And a red wall that symbolized his broken heart.

* * *

Star let herself into her condo. She was home. Home. She

paused, inhaling deeply, disappointed that the new smells didn't smell quite so new anymore.

She set her bag down and went to her phone. The message light blinked. One missed call. Her heart sped up. Hoping against hope the call was from Cade, she pressed the button.

"Star, it's me," Destiny's voice sang out. "Guess who got married?" Her mother laughed. "That's right, it's me. John and I got married yesterday, just a small ceremony in his backyard. I wanted to invite you girls, but, well, we were just impulsive, no time to plan. I got my man, honey. Just as soon as I'm settled, I want you and your sisters to come up and help us celebrate. Be a love and call your sisters for me and give them the news. Bye, sweetie."

The line went dead.

Disgusted, her stomach churning, Star picked up the phone to call Brandi but immediately changed her mind. She wasn't going to be her mother's messenger. She didn't want to field all the questions, didn't want to analyze Destiny and her warped sense of romance.

Right now, she wanted to lick her own wounds.

Star curled up on her bed, missing Cade. She'd botched things up with him. He probably hated her now, and it was her own fault. She finally fell asleep around midnight, her dreams wild and terrifying. Babies floated through her nightmares, crying, reaching for her.

Star woke with a start, her body drenched in sweat.

She got up and went to the bathroom.

She sat on the toilet, and that's when she noticed.

She had her period.

No baby. She pressed a hand to her womb, her empty womb. Everything was okay. She was okay. Her life was perfect, right?

Calmer now, she went back to bed, but she didn't sleep, not for a long, long time.

CHAPTER TWENTY

Exactly ten weeks after they'd shot Cade's home makeover for *Update This!* the show aired.

Star was in front of her TV, so starved to see Cade, his house, his family, she could hardly stand it. She dreamed of babies nearly every night, and she wasn't sure if the dreams were God's way of punishing her, or God's way of signaling her that she wasn't done with Cade yet.

She only knew her life here wasn't enough for her anymore. Even her promotion couldn't cheer her. Her time with Cade and his family had changed her, yet fear kept her in Seattle. She'd hurt Cade and pushed him away more times than she could count. Would he push her away if she asked for another chance?

Star's eyes were drawn to the fireplace mantel, to the painting hanging on the wall above. The landscape of Seward, painted by Patsy, had become her solace, her touchstone. More than ever she wanted to return to Alaska. Maybe she was a hometown girl after all. And she could no longer deny that she was hopelessly in love with a hometown boy.

The show came on, and there he was, every gorgeous inch of him from his dark hair to his sky blue eyes. Her pulse jumped. Her hand went to her stomach, to her empty womb. She'd been mourning the loss of a baby that had never been conceived for ten weeks now.

She'd fallen in love with Cade.

And she'd blown it—big time.

Her phone rang.

Star picked up the call. "Hello?"

"Hey, it's me, Brandi."

"Hi, Bran," Star said, the sound of her sister's voice lightening her mood immediately. "How are you, kiddo?"

"Great. I just watched the show."

"Me, too," Star said. "What did you think?"

"It was wonderful. I wish you could have been here to watch it with me."

"Me, too," Star said, although she wasn't entirely sure she meant the words. "How's everyone?"

"We're all good. Will is growing like a weed."

"Bud?"

"Is fine. Aren't you going to ask me about Cade?"

Star's heart skipped a beat at the mention of his name. "How is he?"

"In fine form. He's hired a nanny. Do you remember Amber McClain? Talk in town is she's after Cade. And I heard from Bud that Cade has mowed down Patsy's."

Star's stomach hit her feet. He'd erased her from his life. He really was done with her.

"Star? Are you there?" Brandi asked.

"Yes."

"I know you love him," Brandi said gently. "Don't bother to deny it. Get your butt up here and fight for your man."

"It's too late," Star said her fingers tightening on the phone. "Trust me. He doesn't want anything to do with me."

"Maybe, but you'll never know for sure if you don't try," Brandi said. "Take a risk, Star." Will's soft cries filled the space between them. "Look, I have to go. Will's up. You haven't responded to my invite for Thanksgiving. I hope you're coming."

"I haven't decided." The pretty orange and brown invite glared at her from the refrigerator.

"It's Will's first Thanksgiving and I want you here with us. Ruby Sue, Tawney, and Mom and John are coming. I want a big family Thanksgiving for my son. Come for Will, Star."

Did Brandi even realize how dysfunctional an event like that would be? They'd need to swill martinis like rock stars just to get through it.

"Say yes, Star," Brandi coaxed. Will's fussing grew louder.

"I'll think about it," Star said. "Go take care of your baby."

"Okay," Brandi agreed and Star could imagine her rocking from side to side, trying to quiet Will. The image sent a rush of longing for her sister through Star. "Bye, Star. Hope to see you soon."

The line went dead. Star set the phone down.

Brandi had just given her a reason to go home.

Did she want to go? Was Cade worth the risk? Yes, her heart sang. Yes.

She was going to Alaska for Thanksgiving.

* * *

"I'm sick of you moping around," Ron said. "Do something about it. Go and get her and bring her back."

Cade glanced up from the reel he was working on. "Mind your own business."

"You've been oiling that same reel for ten minutes. Snap out of it."

"Shut up." Cade tossed the reel on the workbench. He'd been upset since that damned show had aired last night. Watching it had brought back his last days with Star. He couldn't stop thinking about her, about their situation.

"I heard from Bud that she's coming for Thanksgiving."

"What?" Cade asked, his heart kick-starting in his chest.

"Yeah, she's staying at Brandi's. Make up with her. You know you want to."

"Don't you think I've thought about it?" Cade asked. "Butt out. I know what I'm doing."

"You're being stupid," Ron said with a shake of his head. "She loves your kids, anyone can see that. She's scared. Be the bigger man." He walked away, leaving Cade alone.

Cade frowned. He didn't know what to think anymore. And he could hardly stand to go in the kitchen. The place was one big, red reminder of her.

He'd left Star alone long enough. He loved her, and he was going to make sure she knew just how much. Then, if she turned him away, he'd let her go, but he had to give it one more chance.

* * *

Star stood in the O'Brien driveway.

The windows of the old Victorian were filled with golden light. A blanket of snow covered the house, making it look enchanted, welcoming, and warm.

What was Cade doing? Was he carving the Thanksgiving turkey? Were the kids running wild? Was baby Daniel crying, or was he nursing at Trudy's breast?

Images flew through Star's mind as she started forward. She'd left her own family's Thanksgiving at Brandi's to see Cade.

She prayed he wouldn't throw her out when he heard what she had to say.

Star rang the doorbell, the chime making her nerves jump.

Laughter seeped out through the door as Finn's and Emma's footsteps drew near. The door opened.

"Star!" Emma cried.

"Emma." Star went down on her knees. Finn joined them in the group hug. Star's chest tightened with an emotion so powerful she wondered how she ever could have thought of shutting these kids out of her life.

"I've missed you guys," she said.

"I missed you, too," Emma said, pulling away.

"Dad!" Finn shouted. "Star's here."

Star pushed to her feet just as Cade appeared. When he saw her, he stopped. She tried to read the emotion in his eyes but failed.

"Kids, go and tell Trudy to set another place for dinner,"

Cade said.

Finn and Emma ran off to the kitchen, shouting, "Star's here. Star's here."

Cade came toward her. She ached for him, prayed he wouldn't turn her away. Where did she begin? How did she apologize for everything she'd put him through?

When he reached her, he didn't speak. Instead, his arms came around her, and then he was kissing her. Giddy relief washed through Star and she kissed him back, needing this, needing him, not allowing herself to think about what would follow. His kiss made her whole again.

"Gross," Brad said with disgust from the hallway.

They broke the kiss, but Cade's arms tightened around her.

"Star!" Trudy cried, as she rushed from the kitchen, nearly running over Brad. Ron, Finn, and Emma followed until the foyer was crowded with O'Briens, all of them talking at once.

Cade let go of her as Star was passed from O'Brien to O'Brien until she'd hugged them all.

"We were just about to have dinner," Trudy said, her voice rising above the chatter. "I'll set you a place."

"I ate at Brandi's," Star said. "My whole family is there. But don't let me keep you from your dinner. I can come back later."

"No." Cade's fingers closed around hers. "Stay."

"Really?" she asked, afraid to hope.

"I insist." He turned to Ron. "Hold the turkey. Give us a minute."

"Come on, kids," Ron said, spreading his arms wide in an attempt to corral everyone and lead them back to the kitchen. "Let's get the food on the table."

One by one the O'Briens shuffled away.

"Come on," Cade said, tugging on her hand.

Star didn't budge. "No, wait."

He stopped. "What is it?"

"I have to tell you something."

"Tell me."

Star looked into his eyes. "That day, when we took the pregnancy test, well, I know I said I was relieved when I wasn't pregnant. The truth is, I wanted that baby. I wanted your baby. I just didn't know it at the time. I've been a mess ever since."

Cade smoothed her hair. "I wanted that baby, too, but for different reasons. I wanted a tie to you, one that couldn't be broken. It was selfish of me, especially since I knew you didn't want that."

Star's throat closed with emotion. "I want a family." Star touched him this time, her palms against his chest, his heart beating under her right hand. "I've been mourning you and your kids. I love all of you. I can't do it anymore. I know I'm risking my heart, but I want to take the risk. I need to know, do I still have a chance with you?"

"Yes!" Cade picked her up, swinging her around. He kissed her. "I've missed you."

Star kissed him back, growing serious. "I love you," she whispered against his mouth. "So very much."

"I love you, too." Cade smiled. "Come on." He led her outside. "I have something to show you."

"Where are we going?"

"You'll see." His hand closed around hers, and together they ran through the swirling snow toward Patsy's place. When they broke through the trees, Star saw a footing had been poured. Snow covered most of it, but there was a definite footprint of a house outlined in the snow.

"Brandi said you demolished Patsy's place. I figured you were trying to exorcise me."

"Hardly." He laughed. "I leveled it to build your dream house, a house complete with a giant home office."

"What?" She looked at him. "My dream house? I thought Trudy and Ron were going to live here."

"Plans change. Trudy won't leave the new kitchen." Cade pulled her into his arms, hugging her close. "I want to give you a home, Star. A real home of your own. I want to give it to you with no strings attached. I want to build it for you because I'm crazy in love with you."

"Even after everything I said about not wanting kids or a husband?"

"You can push me away all you want, but I'm not going anywhere. We'll find a way to make it work. Love is about compromise. If we have to split our time between two cities, I'm okay with that. Winters are slow here. We can make it work. And summers, well, I wanted to make a place for you, where you could work from here if you wanted to. I don't expect you to be a full-time mom to my kids. I know how important your work is. I can be there for them when you aren't and vice versa."

"You darling man," Star said with wonder. "My life is here, with you. I've thought about this, a lot. I'm an associate producer now. I think I can talk Frank into letting me telecommute part of the time. I'll have to go out of town on location periodically, but for the most part, I think I can make it work."

"Whatever it takes," Cade said. "I'm behind you one hundred percent."

"I love you, Cade."

"I love you, Starlene White." He gave her hair a playful tug.

Her heart bursting with love, snow falling softly around them, Star kissed him.

And she knew, once and for all, that she was finally home.

JOLEEN JAMES

Award-winning author Joleen James became an Indie author with the launch of her contemporary novel *Falling For Nick*. Since that time, she has released her second and third novels, *Under A Harvest Moon* and *Hometown Star*.

When she's not busy writing, Joleen enjoys spending time with her family at her lakeside home in the beautiful Pacific Northwest. You can find Joleen James at www.joleenjames.com and on Facebook and Twitter.

Made in the USA
Charleston, SC
30 September 2013